Martin!

THE ZEPHYR COLLECTION

SIDEWAYS

Maybe short
Stories will not
be such torture?
Take care!
Annie (Zeph)

THE ZEPHYR COLLECTION

Sideways

ZEPHYR ZYWICK

ISBN: 978-1-3939-3106-5 (Paperback)

All creative works by Zephyr Zywick.
Editing by Annie Morgan.
Printed by Umbrella Imprints in the United States of America.

First printing edition 2020.
zephyrzywick@gmail.com

Dedication

Elizabeth Auwarter, my thoughtful friend and dedicated writing comrade, ally, and advocate.

Bart Baker, my talented screenwriting buddy whose first produced movie actually inspired my 100% dissimilar story "A Good Day to Die."

Booker T. Benford, one of the first people who saw me, believed in me, and never left.

Brian Mooney, a sharp and sensitive amigo. Kathmandu kept him and I'm still heartbroken.

Bob Saenz, a remarkable friend who's a stellar, working screenwriter, an unexpected novelist, a screenwriting guru, and a selfless coach.

Introduction

Welcome to my second volume, Sideways. It continues a collection of work across various mediums: stories, essays, memoirs, screenplays, poetry, and lyrics. I never write for shock value, but art imitates life. Sometimes, I follow rules. Sometimes, I don't.

A man I dated said he was confused why I was so elementary and ordinary when I was smart enough to use collegiate words, be more sophisticated and more obscure in my writing. He was also confused when I stopped dating him. Sorry, not sorry. Hope you enjoyed that tidbit.

Warmest Regards,
Zephyr Zywick

Table of Contents

Sideways

A Little Tokyo Drift

Tokyo

Finn's favorite author was Ellie Daniels, but she was a known recluse, or more accurately, a little-known recluse. In fact, most readers didn't know that the famous author Ilsa Blaine was Ellie Daniels writing under her pen name, having discreetly paid tribute to the two main characters from Casablanca by combining their names.

Finn understood her pen name's meaning and that she was hard to get to know. She made public appearances sparingly, lived in the mountains of

Montana, and avoided publicity like the plague.

Ellie was in Tokyo because a famous writer named Naruto Mashimoto had asked her to do the foreword for his upcoming book. That would give them both attention and greater credibility. This would have been easy to handle on paper, but he was very formal and old-school, very busy, and had requested an in-person meeting and interview with her. It made no sense to her, but sometimes life was like that.

As reclusive as she chose to be within the states, Ellie did enjoy traveling the globe and visiting world-famous cities as well as hidden cultural gems.

Online, she had found this oddball little hotel. It was off of a really busy street and the bungalows went straight back in a row from there: one through seven. Seven was her suite, the only suite. As she walked along the breezeway, the doors were on the left and an odd mirror-like wall softly blanketed the angled building on the right, which was only about ten or so feet away. She loved the fact that these rooms all looked like bungalows from the Golden Age of the Sixties in Hollywood. It had filled her with a warm nostalgia when she'd come across them on the travel website, and she'd felt she had to book there.

She had no idea, at that time, that Mr. Mashimoto felt it was his duty to book her a room during her visit and had done so. Somewhere else. Somewhere ordinary.

Once she'd found out, it was too late, and she called her bungalow people to cancel her reservation. The management company who handled a bunch of places, including this quirky one, was forty-five minutes away from the bungalows. Ellie was only here for two days, and she hated to lose all that time returning the key. It was already upsetting her that she would miss staying there.

The manager agreed to allow her to open room seven, set the key on the table, and he would have someone from Housekeeping return it to him later.

That's where she was headed.

As Ellie passed the numbered bungalows, one by one, she was taken aback to see Finn James clearly show up on the mirrored wall on the right, walking a ways behind her, but catching up with his longer, even strides. There was no mistaking that it was Finn. His face had graced magazine covers and billboards for decades. It had sold cars, cologne, movie tickets, glamour, glitz, and gore. He had one of the most recognizable faces on the globe.

She passed room five and he did, too. She could barely breathe, having been a long-time fan of his work since her teen years. She didn't want to look like some ordinary, crazed lunatic, all excited to meet him, but didn't want to miss the opportunity either.

She thought as quickly as she could. Three scenarios played out in her quick mind, and three seconds remained to make a snap decision. She had to muster up every ounce of courage that a soft-spoken, near shut-in could find.

Turning left, abruptly, in front of the door labeled *six,* she slid her key into the lock as Finn almost ran her over.

She spoke up first.

"I'm sorry, I didn't—"

He laughed, "It's fine. I stopped in time. No harm done." He paused, for almost too long of a moment, which felt a little odd. He stared at the door, then at her, and the silence hung in the air. It was palpable.

"So," he spoke up again, running his fingers through his hair, "you're in six, also?" She pulled the key back from the door and slipped it discreetly into her pocket, looking up directly into friendly eyes.

She said, "I can call them. It's not a problem." He easily waved this idea off.

"No, no, don't worry." He laughed again, warm, good-naturedly. "We'll figure it out."

He put his key in the lock, opened the door for both of them, and motioned her in. "My name's Finn. I'll give management a call."

Ellie didn't budge.

He looked her up and down, maybe confused, and said, "You have your flight bag. You're out of breath. Are you just arriving from the airport?"

She nodded.

He spoke again, kid gloves on, adept enough to know how to reassure someone who was shy and uneasy. "I just was in Kyoto for a few days. You must feel the need to freshen up if you just flew over.

That's a long flight into Tokyo. Feel free to shower and change, and I'll make a call to management and see where they can move me."

She came into the bungalow with some hesitation.

He was so calm, as if this made perfect sense, as if any woman should be at ease to walk into a hotel room with another guest over a bit of confusion or maybe as if any woman should be at ease to walk into a hotel room with him? She didn't know.

She was out of breath, true, but only because she had recognized him immediately and she was behaving completely out of character for her. She'd had roughly seven seconds to identify, clarify, classify, and make a bit of an impulsive, irresponsible decision. She hadn't figured out the part about what might happen next.

She said, "I'm not sure—"

He stopped her worried tone and interrupted.

"I'm not leaving you in the street. I hope you're not leaving me there? Did I say I'm Finn? Finn James. Nice to meet you…" He held out his hand.

"Ellie. It's Ellie."

He thought to himself, *Her real name, first name only, not her famous pen name.* Since he didn't miss that detail, he'd have to play dumb. He couldn't act as if he recognized her name from just Ellie.

He nodded and they shook.

"You are American, right?"

She was struggling mentally for a story to manufacture. It was obvious he would wonder what rock she must have been living under if she didn't know he was *Finn*. For being a professional storyteller, she was sucking royally at this.

"Yes, American. I live in Montana. I'm here meeting a client about um… a…

work-type project. I'm only here for a couple of days."

"Are you all right?" He pushed for information just a little bit. "Something's wrong. Are you upset? Do I seem familiar or something?"

"Recognize you?" She about choked on her words. He'd asked if he *seemed familiar*, not if she recognized him.

He tried not to laugh noticeably at her awkwardness. She was completely adorable. She yammered on, "I mean, no, I'm not upset. And I don't, nope. Not offhand." She faded off a bit. "I'm sorry. I don't keep up, really." Wow, what a mess of words that was.

He thought, S*he might have just topped the charts for the most awkward display of a fan trying to casually play off recognizing me.*

"No worries, Ellie. You're good."

He acted satisfied with that and motioned her to the bathroom, where she pulled in her bag, locked the door, breathed a few times, and decided freshening up was not a bad idea for myriad reasons.

Outside that door, Finn was left scratching his head.

He stared at the locked door for a moment, then heard the water turn on. He quietly moved to the main bungalow door and let himself outside. He looked at *his* key. It said MASTER.

He began pacing up and down the sidewalk and muttering out loud, half laughing, completely lost. He said the most unexpected thing to the empty breezeway.

"Why did she go to room six? What the hell? She was supposed to go to the suite, to seven, to return her key. The manager gave me a master key to hold me, because he could trust me. Now, she's in six, without a key to six, hopping into the shower." He shook his head.

"I'm in six, without a key to six, pacing outside. Someone who hasn't arrived yet is booked in six and nobody is booked in seven, which is the only suite. This is crazy."

Luckily, no one heard that little rant. "Fate, don't fail me now," he half yelled at the sky.

The street got noisy.

He moved his thoughts to inside his head as he leaned his back against the door.

There was no way she couldn't have recognized me. The color draining from her face when I asked if I seemed familiar kind of drove that point home, but she wouldn't let herself admit it aloud. She was exasperating. Okay, okay. This all could work out for him.

He knew Ellie Daniels rarely left her compound. By the time he'd found out her travel plans and flown in, she had already changed plans and was switching hotels. His perfect way to meet his favorite reclusive writer, which was maybe a tiny bit stalkerish, had suddenly shifted to a room number in a hotel that neither of them had even reserved. Unbelievable.

He heard wheels rolling and looked over. A couple walked towards him with small rolling bags. He ran up to them, almost praying. They looked a bit scared by his rapid approach.

"Are you in room six, by chance?" He held up his key and motioned for them to do the same. It did not look like they spoke a word of English. They held up their key, also. A number "6" was etched into it.

Finn was excited. "Yes!"

He pulled out his phone and touched the translator app. He pressed 'English to Japanese' and spoke, then held it up for them. In Japanese, it said:

"Here is a key that will work for suite seven. It's much nicer than the small room six. No more money. No more cost. It's a gift from management. Please exchange your key with me and accept your beautiful gift." He nodded to them, motioning down the sidewalk, hoping the next five minutes was not going to consist of them finding out their paid-for room came equipped with a woman in the shower.

The couple nodded up and down and looked very excited at getting a better room for no more money, no more cost. The woman grabbed their key out of her husband's hand and traded Finn very happily and quickly. They bowed back and forth to Finn too many times, then moved on down the sidewalk to the suite. *Yes,* he thought. *Yes*!

Finn quietly re-entered six, his new favorite number, poured a glass of water, and blew out a slow breath. He was already coming at this sideways, but this required degree of finesse was unexpected. He smiled to himself. *This might work.* Then, *Why? Why am I going to this much trouble?*

Ellie stepped out into the room wearing different clothes, really attractive ones, all freshened up, and looking a bit apprehensive. *This. This was why.* He sighed.

He realized he had to reassure this adorable woman and get her to relax before she imploded. She was out of her element and could still easily spook and bolt out of here.

The manager had privately divulged the story of why seven was opening up again. Finn knew she had the Mashimoto reservation to save her, as well as the key to seven, which now had a new couple in it.

He told himself, *Don't worry.* It was all going better than he'd expected his non-plan of a plan to go anyway, but this was still a potential powder keg.

He spoke up: friendly, unassuming, approachable, "I called management. There should be someone checking out within a few hours. If you haven't eaten, we could walk somewhere… together… get a bite to eat, kill some time. I could leave my bag here until they move me… if it's okay."

"Oh, I can move. It's fine." She blurted that out, then looked at the floor. *It wasn't like she didn't have another room lined up.*

He chuckled.

"Whichever. Let's figure it out later on. You know, I could eat. How about you?" He gave his best *I'm not a serial killer* smile, and it worked.

They locked up the bungalow and meandered slowly towards the insanely busy street. Nightlife was just beginning to pick up. Everyone and everything moved at the speed of light, except them.

They ambled along slowly, chatting, relaxed, since all of their lies were out of the way. They had nothing more to fear and fell back into a level of comfort reserved for people who knew each other really well. From a distance, they looked like an old black-and-white movie, playing in slow motion, while the city moved around them like a full-color, lit-up highway.

Finn knew she loved sushi from an interview he'd seen, couldn't tell her he knew, so he asked her. She confirmed, yes, she did love sushi. Eventually, he led her into a sushi restaurant and took great care to spend hours savoring an enjoyable meal together, slowing time down to a crawl, getting her laughing, talking about everything in the world, except what he did for a living and what she did for a living.

By the time they returned to the room around midnight, it seemed as natural as could be to gently press her against the door and kiss the top of her head. No hurry here. He didn't want to scare her off. He kissed her cheek and moved slowly left to find exactly what he'd hoped to find, her lips rising to meet his in a kiss that was genuine, tender, and perfectly timed.

She had to follow his lead.

For one thing, after getting to know him for the past twenty-something years, and then after getting to *know* him for the entire evening… She didn't *want* to walk away. At this moment, she knew she'd made the right call with the key. And she was right where she wanted to be.

For another thing, the key she had in her pocket was to room seven.

His key was easy to find.

The door was easy to open.

He moved his fingers deep into her hair and smiled, then put his arms around her and reined it in. He stood there, a bit worried that if he was pushing this too forcefully, she might push back. As if in answer to that, she took his hands, and walked backward a few steps into the room, pulling him in.

Ahh, okay.

It was also easy to fall into bed together.

Finn did know he'd never asked management a damn thing about check-outs and he'd done an admirable job at keeping her from inquiring about it when they'd returned to the room. He still hadn't quite wrapped his head around the idea that Ellie, by inserting her key into the wrong room, was indicating that she had no interest in any other rooms opening up later on.

A voice inside his head said, Finn... she didn't return her key and she didn't go wherever she was supposed to go that Mr. Mashimoto had reserved. So, there's that.

Just in case she wasn't convinced enough by his incredible efforts to distract her from leaving, he did an admirable job of continuing to keep it off her mind, again, around four-thirty in the morning.

Eight o'clock came a bit too soon, but he felt as happy as he'd been in a long time. He nudged her awake.

"Do I have crazy hair?" She looked genuinely worried, trying to blindly straighten it.

He laughed and said, "Pick a coffee. On your left is cream and sugar. Right is black."

"Cream and sugar, please." She reached for the correct one.

He handed it over. "Thank you, God," he said, overly relieved.

She burst out laughing. "What if I'd said 'black' to you?"

"Then, I would have suffered a terrible injustice." He motioned over to his laptop bag. "I have to meet some produ— well, production, I mean... product specialists about something in the city. I'll be back by two at the latest, I think."

She was painfully aware she had no key and was stuck in her crazy lies again. However, she had just witnessed him awkwardly struggle to *not* talk about what he did for a living. Playing dumb seems to have been the right answer, seems to have been what he wanted or needed or responded to? Well, as to the time, two might be okay. She had no idea but had to make it work, regardless.

"That's fine," she said, "I have to go meet with a gentleman named Naruto for the work project." She paused and decided to see where he stood. "He messaged me, though. It, um, turns out he also booked me a room, if you want me to—"

Finn interrupted, "No, you'll be back. Right? Tonight?"

"I can be, unless… I understand if you want me to accept the open room."

Oh my God. She didn't make it easy, did she?

He had to spell it all out.

He guessed it was a good thing, though. It showed him she wasn't sure if it had been a one-night stand, a random hookup on his part. She was being kind enough to give him an *out*. That was actually sweet.

The furthest thing on his mind was having an out, but she was offering one. He looked at her, a little worried with her furrowed brow, and he kissed the top of her head again. He didn't know what scent caught his attention, but she smelled really good.

He said, "The last thing I want for you to do is take another room at this point. I feel like whatever has happened in the past twenty-four hours has been one of the luckiest, most serendipitous, wacky things in my life, but I wouldn't take back a moment. And I'm looking forward to a lot more moments, unless *you* want—"

This time, Ellie interrupted in her soft-spoken way, "I can meet you back here after two, then. I'd like that very much, Finn."

He'd done it. She was reassured. She was a lot of work, but it was more satisfying than all the ones who were effortless, for whatever that was worth.

That afternoon, she showed up and knocked. He opened the door and laughed.

"Yes? Lose your key?"

Deny. Deny. Deny.

"No, it's in my pocket, but I didn't want to startle you. You might have been… indisposed."

He laughed out loud.

"I was not, but now that you are here, should we go eat or should we become indisposed?"

He slipped his arms around her and leaned down to give her a much warmer hello with a kiss.

He was hungry, but also, he was *hungry*. He was good with either decision to be made, here.

Afternoon and night number two was more, more of everything. More food, more banter, more lovemaking, more exciting, but also more comfortable.

Late in the night, they were like teenagers in the shower, playing, smiling, laughing. Nothing about her seemed triggered. No shyness. No weird starstruck face, thank God. The only thing wrong with describing the moment as *perfect* was how overused that word was. The only thing wrong with the word *comfortable* was it implied a lack of excitement and passion, also wrong.

He'd been with so many partners over the years that this encounter should have been nothing all that special. Maybe, it was the reversal of it. He wasn't the hunted one. He wasn't being chased or coveted or treated like a commodity or a trophy. Once that moment of awkwardness was gone, it was clear, he wasn't on some weird pedestal. She saw him, not his persona.

He'd liked her work. It had started there. He'd looked her up, watched what few video interviews she'd done, read some written interviews, etc. He had become, over time, impressed with the person she was, with what she said, and maybe it *was* kind of interesting how much she rejected fame.

She didn't hate people, but she didn't seek the spotlight, the glory, the whole circuit that came with being a celebrity. She lived a quiet life, a notably charitable life, and her views, so far, had seemed pretty aligned with his.

It had been a little bit breathtaking. He'd made a few calls, developed his own little safe-but-enticing obsession, maybe slipped a few bucks to a travel agent to teach him how to look up travel plans on the agent's company computer, and maybe slipped him a few more bucks to look away while he looked up a few things on said-company-computer.

Tokyo, it turned out, and she was leaving right away. That was unexpected, but okay. Intriguing. It had gone from there and had taken a few odd turns. He thought about all of this as he ran his hands over her back and down her waist, rinsing the soap away.

She leaned up and kissed him. She. Kissed. Him. That made her think. Usually, she wasn't one to take the initiative. She responded just fine but didn't usually *step up*. Yet, she just had. She was still figuring out her behavior of suddenly turning left and putting seven into six's door. She'd instantly seen three scenarios. One was bad, no chance to speak at all. Why, in just an instant, had she had a feeling it would all work out all right? She shrugged.

"What?" he asked.

"I'm sorry?" She looked confused.

"You sighed, Ellie. You're thinking about something." She floundered a bit but opted for the truth...ish.

"Um, I was thinking… I'm trying to figure out exactly how I ended up naked, in the shower with you, with bubbles running down my back and soap in my hands and rubbing your chest and... I'm thinking, I really want to rinse off because I want this to move back to the bed, again... And then,

I'm thinking, I'm freaking out a little that I just said all of that out loud."

He smiled and laughed a good-natured laugh. He really liked honesty and people who didn't filter every word, and except for their little bit of mutual lying, they really came at each other pretty raw and honestly. As they rinsed off and kissed, he pressed her against the wall, and she slipped slightly. He caught her, but it startled him. Finn turned off the water and reached for the towel. He decided they could get hot and bothered in a much safer spot than this.

He made sure they did.

Every time they had been together so far, it was slightly different. Ever evolving. More intense. More relaxed. More twisted up in the covers. More open, no covers at all. It had been two days. This was the fourth time, and he was captivated.

Morning was coming too soon. Their final morning. This was hitting him.

After passing the most recent advance in their evolutionary cycle, lying on his back relaxed, he asked her flat out if she could stay in Tokyo with him for a little while longer.

She said, "No, I have animals I had to kennel. I have to get back." He thought for a few minutes and her breathing became more even.

"Maybe I could visit?" He looked at her.

His question dangled in the air, unanswered because she had nestled into his arms, rested her head on his chest and fallen asleep.

The alarm went off at six.

He was carrying two cups of coffee to the bed. Gently he said, "I'm sorry, Ellie, my hands were full."

She shut off the alarm, a bit startled, adorably naked, and accepted her coffee.

"Do I have crazy hair?" she wondered.

He laughed and said, "Only always."

She smiled at that and he asked, "Can I have that bottle in the shower?"

She repeated, "Bottle in the shower?" He laughed aloud at how weird he must have sounded.

"Yeah, it smells good. I like it. It smells like you."

She nodded, smiling, and thought, He probably doesn't recognize the smell because it's a really popular option from Dollar Tree.

She said, "It's called Coconut Water Mist. I just put some into a small spray bottle for travel. You are welcome to have it."

He grabbed it and stuck it in his bag as they both got up, got dressed. Then everything got lined up, and all of it ready to go by the door.

His face turned serious. "I really am not ready for you to go. Stay longer."

She slipped her arms around his neck. "I don't want to go yet. I had a g… I had the b..." she searched for the words. "Finn, it's been amazing. Every moment."

"I could call you? I have a phone, you know. I could email. Visit you in Montana," he added.

She looked at him doubtfully and said, "My life is boring and uneventful. It's quiet, except for the animals, of which I have two horses, a goat, three dogs, four cats, and a rabbit. All rescues. I live in the middle of nowhere."

He pictured it. "You don't know how good that sounds." He kissed her nose and paused. "I live in the middle of everywhere. Sometimes, that's been a difficult choice."

A honk sounded. It was time.

He said, "Oh, you can leave your key. I'll return it for you. I leave late this afternoon."

She slipped the key out of her pocket and laid it face down on the table, as she leaned up and hugged him tightly. He seemed distracted by that move. *Score.*

"I have to go," she said.

"I know. I know." He sighed and smiled, grabbed the handle of her bag and walked her to the waiting car.

She said, "I do want to say yes, but everything about saying yes scares me."

He kissed her hair and held her close.

The taxi driver looked annoyed, but before complaining, decided maybe this was going to be pretty hot to watch. Neither Finn nor Ellie noticed he was a bit nosy, albeit harmless.

Finn nodded at her fear, resigned, thinking ahead, but letting it go for now.

"I understand, Ellie." She changed the subject.

"I found a tourist shop on the way back from my meeting yesterday. I bought a couple of trinkets."

That was random.

"Okay?" He said, puzzled.

"I left you one. I guess it's silly. I'm a Casablanca fan."

"It's not silly. That's sweet. Casablanca?"

"We'll always have Paris?" She quoted the film.

"We're in Tokyo."

She acknowledged, "I didn't say it made a lot of sense." He laughed out loud. She was quirky. He liked quirky.

In all earnestness, he said, "Thank you."

The taxi driver was now impatient. No, they weren't being hot enough.

"Lady, come on."

Again, one more kiss.

They were so connected. He felt it. She felt it.

Her mind was telling her, It was just this moment in time. They couldn't sustain this.

"Okay, " he said and stepped back.

"Okay, Finn."

She nodded and settled into the car. He shut the door and waved her off. As the taxi drove up the street, she fought off the tears of her cowardice. *What's wrong with me*?

He walked back to his room and realized he saw himself in the mirrored wall as he went. He'd never paid attention to that before. Ellie had been quite the distraction.

As he walked into the room, he saw the key. It was attached to a little keychain with a miniature Eiffel Tower. Or Tokyo Tower. Well, Tokyo *did* have its own Tokyo Tower that was nearly identical. He started to take the ring off the key, then turned the key over.

Etched on it was the number seven.

He sat down, leaned way back, and lost himself in thought and he spun the keychain around on his finger. She didn't conveniently forget to leave the key, so he'd never know. She left the seven, fully aware that he would see it.

Right?

Ellie never did know that Finn was never assigned six, but she was basically admitting that she, herself, was never assigned six.

Wasn't she? Maybe, this changed everything.

He thought that he had been employing a little *Tokyo Drift*, using a Fast and Furious phrase, coming at this whole situation a little bit sideways, with kid gloves, some minor misdirection, and a deft touch.

But she left the seven key and even added a trinket to it. It called out for attention.

He thought about what he'd just seen. The mirrored wall. She had been walking ahead of him. What if she'd seen him, known she was assigned seven, and figured the only one left for him to be in was six? Was that why she stopped suddenly?

Wait, had she put the seven key into the six slot, knowing it wouldn't work?

Best case scenario for her? She'd pull the key back out, all concerned, and allow him to be the hero and share the room? Really? Possible?

Worst case scenario, he'd pass her because he'd already booked seven. Then she'd follow, apologizing for accidentally stopping one short. She'd return her key, explaining, and maybe they'd hit it off. Her best and her worst-case scenario… both of them were face to face, sorting something out together.

No, wait, that was wrong. That wasn't the best/worst case scenario. That was the best case/best case scenario. She was a professional writer. She had run through these outcomes faster than he could have known they existed. There weren't two options. There were three.

Worst case scenario? She went all the way to seven to return the key. He let himself into six and closed the door on them getting to meet at all. She couldn't guarantee meeting him if she walked to seven.

All three scenarios only made sense if—she had seen him and recognized him in the mirrored wall, adapted accordingly, and damn fast.

Then, she'd played dumb. That was fine. He understood that because he had played dumb, too. Maybe, she imagined he would like a moment in his life *not* to be recognized. That was thoughtful. She *was* thoughtful. That worked. But that wasn't what was nagging him. She recognized him, didn't say so, but what else? What was nagging away?

The key! That was it. The key was the key. She could have just turned towards him and said she'd seen him in the mirror, and it was a pleasure to make his acquaintance. She hadn't.

She had put her seven key into six, as if it were her room. At that moment, he had been at such a loss as to *why* she did it and decided six was his only option, too. He couldn't process so quickly, *What if I continue to seven, where I was headed*?

All the confusion aside, the bottom line was, when she saw him and assessed they might be side by side or switching out the same room, her only way of finding out and innocently meeting him, was to do what she had done. She would have won either way. Her only way to lose would have been to keep walking and take a chance. It boggled his mind.

This was why he liked her writing. She was wicked smart. It had taken him approximately two hours at this table, two days after the fact, to figure out what she had done in about ten footsteps.

He smiled, putting it all together. The second she'd seen him, she'd wanted to meet him, but as accidentally as he'd wanted to accidentally meet her. She didn't *just* recognize him. She was a fan. She was attracted to him. He was already on her radar.

He shook his head with a smile as he thought about how they could have had a really nice suite.

He smiled and pocketed the number seven key and the keychain as a memento. Management could make new ones.

His bag was ready to go. His car was waiting.

He looked into the room from the doorway and thought, *This is nothing like the rooms I rent, the suites I reserve. I stay in the best of the best, mostly for security. This place is so quirky, like Ellie, I guess. It's like some old Hollywood bungalow from fifty years ago. There was barely a full bed for us. The decor looks like it hasn't been updated since 1962.*

He looked at the light beaming in through the half-open shutter windows and thought, *It's like this place is frozen in time, like the last two days were frozen in time, like time got bent. Sideways. But it's the best time-bender I've ever had.*

One last look, one last breath, and he pulled the door to a close, walked to the car, and handed his bag to the driver.

His jet had been fueled and was waiting. He knew just a simple change of plans could direct him to Montana, but he stared out the window, thinking, *Not yet. Montana's not going anywhere. I'm going to have to come up with a plan.*

Beyond content, lost in thought, he leaned his head back in the seat, propped up his feet, and closed his eyes as his private plane quietly crossed the Pacific and headed for home. A plan was forming.

Seattle

Two months later, the new book release by Ilsa Blaine provided him an opening in a small Seattle bookstore. At four o'clock, he stood in line wearing a shapeless jacket, a ball cap, sunglasses, and a fake beard.

The table opened up and he set Ilsa Blaine's book down for an autograph, but before she could open it up to sign it, he placed a keychain on top of it. A miniature Eiffel Tower was attached and, beside it, was a miniature Big Ben clock tower charm.

She immediately understood who was standing before her but was still confused.

Slowly, taking a deep breath, she looked up as he pulled down his sunglasses.

She spoke quietly.

"Big Ben? We haven't been to London, Finn." He shrugged.

"We haven't been to Paris, either. It doesn't have to make sense. Ilsa." He used her pen name in public. He knew.

The crowd was stirring behind him. He smiled as Ellie took a labored breath, all of their secrets and lies gone.

"Do you like sushi," she asked as if she didn't know.

"I do." He played along. "I know a place that's closer than a plane ride, if you're interested."

She smiled and looked resolute. Opening the front cover of her new release, she wrote for a good minute, then placed it into his hands as the small crowd behind him became more restless.

He nodded, smiled, and pushed his sunglasses back up.

Walking away discreetly, a person in line started to say, "Hey, aren't you Fi…"

But he casually turned and walked away from the fan and from the bookstore. Safely outside and hidden away in his nondescript rental, he opened the cover of the book.

Above the title, it said, "Finn: The book signing ends at six, not seven. Make sure you get the number right. If you haven't eaten, we could walk somewhere… together. I know I could eat. How about you?"

Below the title, it said, "Thank you for showing up, for coming back, and of course for New York City." He laughed. "Yours. Truly. Ilsa Blaine."

Nothing was lost on him—not the allusion to Casablanca in her pen name, not the words she repeated back from their first night before dinner, not the play on words with six and seven, not the punctuation of *yours truly.* Every word, always meaning something.

Wicked smart. She was wicked smart.

Finn drove down the block, putting distance between the shop and his rearview mirror. It was all good, though. He knew he would see Ellie in less than two hours.

For now, he just had to hit up his GPS and find out what sushi restaurants were around. Maybe, it wouldn't be the worst idea in the world to find a place in Seattle to stay for a night, or two, or a week. Someplace quirky.

Essence

If I shared with you my essence
Opened up and let you in –
Would it be just the beginning
Or the beginning of the end?

If I shared my very spirit
My heart, body, mind, and soul –
Would you do the same intensely
Or would you turn from me and go?

If I let you *see* my essence
Would your eyes be satisfied –
With the binding and the title
And the contents locked inside?

Would you read each page with wonder
As if the words were always new –
Would you trade the dog-eared copy
For a Volume Number Two?

If I let you *hear* my essence
Spoken softly in your ear –
Would it speak the very words
You dreamed you'd someday hear?

Would the echoes touch the places
Where no one had ever gone–
Would their resonance lift you higher
Than any height you'd ever known?

If you *inhaled* my small essence
A light and subtle scent –
Would you inhale me deeply
Then breathe me out again?

Would you like the fragrance?
Would you infuse it with your own –
Would it be the kind of scent that
Warmly, made you think you're home?

If I let you *taste* my essence
Would you discern the subtle taste –
If it's not a sassy salsa
In a jalapeno base?

Would the taste insatiate you?
Would it satisfy your needs –
Could your thirst and hunger
both be quenched
By a woman-child like me?

If I let you *touch* my essence
Would you plumb the depths inside –
With a gentle curiosity
That could never be denied?

Would you venture past those pleasures
To my fragile inner core –
And protect me when I'm vulnerable
Overwhelmed, unsure?

Would you hold at bay each fear I have
Would my heart, for once, be spared –
Would the echoes that can haunt me
Steer clear of what we shared?

My essence can't be taken
And no…
It won't be sold –
But I can give it freely
Or keep it silently on hold.

If a soul exists who has a silver tongue
And nerves of steel –
A heart of gold and head of reason
The ability to feel.

An essence waits in limbo
Not lonely, but alone –
Defending faith in fairy tales
And, too, what dreams I've known.

Hanging in The Balance

Tommy, Age 16

I know I'm only sixteen, but I'm really mature for my age. My friends can see that, but my parents can't. They treat me like a child and get really upset if I have a few beers or smoke a little pot. I told them that I wanted to be an actor, that I'd better start soon and get my foot in the door.

I can always go back to get my GED. When I even mentioned moving out to Hollywood, they balked. They never take me seriously. I just wish they were cool. My dad is the worst.

Anyway, I've got it all planned out. I've been saving up money from my lunch and allowance for months. By spring, I'll have enough money for a bus ticket, and some left over. I only need a few clothes, and I'll pack a lot of food to last me for a while.

When I get to Hollywood, I'll check out the scene, hit all the right places. If I get in good with the stars, I'll always have a place to crash and I'll be able to get my start in movies.

Within a year, I'll write and invite my parents out to visit my new place. I'll show them I was right. You'll see.

Joe, Age 46

Someday soon, I'm going to sit down and write my novel. I was going to start it back in college. I got married, had kids, there's just never enough time in the day. My daughter's in college and I hope my son will be someday soon.

Once things settle down around here, I can really concentrate. I've got it all planned out. I'll get myself organized, buy a new desk, a good office chair, some trays to hold my pens, paper clips, and staples. I'll get it all together.

I've always known I was destined to write a masterpiece and someday I'm going to do it. Oh, yes, someday soon.

Tommy, Age 45

Hollywood just wasn't what I expected it to be. The people weren't that nice. Nobody thought I was special. Nobody could see.

The food in my suitcase didn't last very long. I crashed where I could, but not with any stars. I guess I met some real lowlifes, but at least they noticed me.

When I had nowhere to sleep, I'd lean up against a dumpster and watch for cops. If they found out who I was, they would have sent me home. I watched the back doors of restaurants and went through their trash for leftover food. Some good stuff, even if it was a bit mixed up together.

I survived for many years by performing a trade that I won't speak of here. At least I was drunk or stoned most of the time, so I don't remember all that much.

By the time I turned thirty, my body had deteriorated considerably. Most of my teeth were gone and I was underweight. I had aged beyond my years.

Business had dried up completely by then. There were shelters where I could get a meal, and winters weren't like they'd been in Iowa, so I endured.

The cops never did learn my true identity. Tommy got shortened to Tom-Tom, as I was known to them and everyone else on the street, just like my nickname from childhood.

I was so sure I would make it. Now, I just wait for the end. I know it won't be long.

Joe, Age 67

I was sitting on my bed staring out the window, thinking how much I missed my wife. The doorbell rang. I got up and went to the door.

My granddaughter, Alex, who was sixteen bounced in with her notebook and gave me a big hug.

She was excited because she'd just written a story that she was so proud of and had to tell me about it.

I made some hot tea and she chatted with me about becoming a writer. It was her dream. I smiled to myself. After tea and sugar cookies, she bounded out again with the same energy.

I went back to my bedroom and stared outside until there was only darkness. That night I dreamed. My epiphany came at age sixty-seven, too late for me, but only for me.

The next morning, I fished some paper out of my filing cabinet and scurried around to find a pen. I sat down and wrote Alex a letter.

My dearest Alex,

Your energy and determination always brighten my day. You're so excited about writing, always carrying that journal around with you and writing any new idea in it. You told me your dream is to be a writer. Once, I wanted to be a writer too. I was going to write the Great American Masterpiece.

I was always waiting for the perfect time, the best conditions. I waited too long. I kept putting it off for someday. Someday never came.

Tommy was just the opposite of me. I've never told you about him. It's been something we kept from you to protect you. I think that was a bad decision. You don't need protecting.

Tommy was four years younger than your mother. He ran away from home when she was away at college. He wanted to become an actor. I traced his bus ticket to Hollywood, but every lead eventually turned into a dead end. I always hoped he'd prove me wrong. I always hoped he'd make it. I watched for him in the movies, but I never saw or heard from him again.

Tommy was impulsive. I was the procrastinator. If you're going to be a writer, this is the advice I would give you. Write something every day. Join your school newspaper now and join when you go to college. Research the industry. Know what's expected of you.

Find your voice, and don't let anyone's rejection stop you. Believe in yourself but listen to criticism with an open mind. You don't need the perfect desk or a tray for your paper clips and staples. They come in boxes, use them. But never use the word "someday." It will only steal your dreams.

I love you, Alex.

Granddad

Alex, Age 41

I'm going to start writing my new novel. It's been on the back burner for twenty-two years. When I graduated from college, I got married and had children right away. It was wonderful to stay at home with them and write.

I published many articles on parenting in magazines and published my first children's book when I was twenty-four. I signed on for a series and produced several others over the next two years.

When I was twenty-six, I went to Hollywood. I said it was to research a novel, but that wasn't the truth. My husband was the only one who knew.

I took pictures of Tommy with me and started to research his whereabouts on my own. I'd already called over two hundred phone numbers of the same name with no luck. The private detective I'd hired had come up with nothing.

In Hollywood, the police station produced no results. Tommy did not exist on paper. I went to shelter after shelter, visiting with the homeless and the caregivers.

I asked if there was anyone who'd been there for many years. I struck out time and time again. An old homeless man on the street thought he recognized the picture. He said it looked like Tom-Tom, a vagrant who hung out farther down in the district.

Traveling on foot, I went through many alleys until I found him. But I did find him. He was forty-five, but he looked much older.

I told him who I was and why I came, and he stared at me for a long time. Then his face filled with emotion and he began to cry. I held him in my arms, trying to ignore the stench of the unwashed and comfort this man, my uncle.

I knew I couldn't take him back home in this condition, so I rented a hotel room. He didn't look much better cleaned up, but he smelled better. His health was rapidly failing, and I worriedly got him to a doctor. He was diagnosed with full-blown AIDS. It was in the late stages. It was only a matter of time. Very little time.

I stayed with him for three weeks, we chatted every day. He wasn't strong, but he wanted to talk, to be heard. I listened.

He told me how he'd wanted to be an actor, come out here, become a star. He told me of the world of prostitution, the drugs, the drink, life on the streets.

He insisted I write down everything he said–to publish his story one day. I did as he asked and filled journal after journal with writing, a sad and compelling tale of a life stolen, a dream unrealized.

When death won the battle, I made sure he had a decent burial. I sighed as I turned in the key and headed for home.

Granddad had moved in with us when he was seventy-five, two years before. He had a nice area to himself, and we had our privacy, too. On the plane ride home, I realized I could never tell Granddad the truth. He had two dreams in his life: to become a writer, and to see his son make it after all.

Excited to hear about my visit, I told him of all the places I'd seen and people I'd met. He nervously inquired about Tommy. I told him I never met him, but I did hear of someone by that name who owned a production studio called Tom-Tom pictures. His eyes welled up as he relived a memory.

"I used to call him Tom-Tom when he was just a boy."

I smiled at him as I handed him a cup of hot tea. He seemed so relieved that his son might have proved him wrong. I would never break his heart. I would write the book, as I'd promised, but not until Granddad was gone from this world. He was with us until he was eighty-seven, lively and encouraging, always curious about my work. He was always my first reader, my best editor, my steadfast inspiration. I'm thankful I had him with me until I was thirty-seven.

Four years have passed since he died. My one regret is that I never had the courage to tell him that it was his letter that changed my life.

Each year on his birthday, I go to his gravesite and place a copy of that letter on his gravestone. On the envelope, I write "Thank you, Granddad, I'll love you, always."

One day, when I die, I'll see Granddad again. I'll run right up to him and hold him tightly. I'll have the courage to tell him what his words meant to me. One day, I will let him know he *did* write his masterpiece. It was his letter to me. I would say "someday," but I erased that word from my vocabulary twenty-five years ago. And I never looked back.

The Worst Enemy I've Ever Had

Her appearance was just ostentatious
Her words were mean, unjust, hellacious
She appeared each time I was flying high
To pull me down from the clear blue sky.

In veiled disguise – she could pour on
A smiling manner – an oxymoron.
Underneath she raged with hate
Enjoyed me in weakened state.

All my life, her voice was caustic
She thought herself a wizened Gnostic
She was just a jaded soul
Who never felt she was quite whole.

Her shrill insults were cacophonous
Contorted faces were no bonus.
Mein Enemy – her sobriquet
She couldn't, wouldn't go away.

Her anger spewed like a volcano
Lava poured as does a vein flow.
Every time I was on top
She tried to put it to a stop.

For thirty years she did ensue
I wasn't sure what I would do.
Each dream I had was stolen such
I didn't want them all that much.

I never would be beautiful
I never would be suitable.
I never would become a writer
I wasn't even a worthy fighter.

She picked at me and wore me down
She thrashed my deeds and stole my crown
Her evil ways tormented me
And no one else could even see.

Thirty years I did endure
Her wrath, her lies, her overture
She took my hopes and gave back fears
Did I endure for thirty years?

I told myself – I've had enough
No need to listen to that stuff.
I'm bright, I'm fun, I look just fine
No longer could she undermine.

I took her words and laughed out loud
I told her that she should be proud
I've come so far – through such hard times
My writing has earned several dimes.

I may not be well known or rich
But I still write, I've got the itch.
I may not be living all my dreams
But all is never what it seems.

At least I try – I yelled at her
I offer more than unkind words
When you insult me, you inspire –
Your evil only lifts me higher.

The worst enemy I've ever had
Gasped and finally said – I'm glad.
I looked confused – did I just hear her?
She smiled back from my own mirror.

Sometimes, You Lose

I have such a story to tell you. It's not a good, fun story. It *is* about friendship, lies and betrayal. It's about surprise. Names and places have been changed to protect the innocent, and even... to protect the guilty.

You know, I tuck in my shirts a lot, instead of wearing them *out,* so there's that. Well, I figured I had better start there because I've been told—in no uncertain terms—that it's very much a sign of what a dork I really am, and that's going to become an important point in a little bit.

Growing up, I was a teacher's kid: kind of smart, a little nerdy, with a slight build that always resembled a teenager more than an adult. I was an avid reader. I could get lost in a world where I could be anything, do anything, look any way I wanted. I could solve crimes, experience lives and different time periods vicariously. It was wondrous, exceptional, stellar.

My bedroom was my sanctuary. When people make fun of those who are living in their mom's basement, I laugh. I wasn't doing that. I had my own place. Yet, I could understand the safety that that parents-basement life would provide. Anyway, sometimes I did venture out.

Oh, yes. There was a time, and there was a place.

When I was in my twenties, I had this favorite place to go. It was amazing. An equal playing field for all. Truly humbling, leveling, and elevating all at the same time.

Everyone who showed up there – it didn't matter who you were, where you were from, how you looked, how much money you had, if you were famous or if you were nobody, you were all equalized in one moment. That sounds like it could be a bad thing, but it wasn't at all.

It was the kind of place where everyone who showed up immediately blended into the *moment* without feeling ignored. I have never felt more alive than in that place. I don't even need to close my eyes. I can hear it, smell it, feel the moment and everyone who ventured to that spot surrounding me. I can relive it at will, just by recalling it to memory. Right now, it's taking me back.

As an aspiring artist, I designed a shirt to wear on these occasions. A piece of artwork I'd seen, with an obscure, historic connection to this favorite place in my world. Those in-the-know were impressed, which actually surprised me and, yes, made me feel a little bit special. Those who had no idea of its connotation still liked the shirt without knowing the reference. I was a small-time star. Very small time, but just enough to make me feel great.

On one New Year's Eve, I made plans to go there with an acquaintance, but we arrived too early. Sometimes, when there's a drive involved, and inclement weather, it's hard to judge one's timing. She and I showed up to closed doors and had to hang out in another location that was open down the street. And that's when I met *her*.

It started out innocently enough. She was beautiful, hip, a counter-culture beauty that reminded me of a young Neve Campbell. She was sitting with two friends of her own. She immediately took to me, and our groups combined. The night progressed and we all ended up going to my spot together.

I found out they were all from out of town, as were we. I offered up my hotel room as a night's refuge in the blizzard that had started and the three politely declined in favor of more partying and then driving home after.

Yet, as fate would have it, they showed up at 3 a.m., hoping I would not be angry and would still take them in. This was a no-brainer. Of course. They were trustworthy and, also, that was the *code*. We talked for a few minutes, then the five of us crashed on the two double beds, exhausted. In the morning, I ventured out and brought back doughnuts.

Everyone exchanged numbers and addresses. The girl I'd gone with originally was from Detroit and just visiting me for the week. She was actually pretty mental, but that's another story entirely. Oh my. In this new group, one was from Indiana, so we will call him Indy. The other two were from Ohio. I will refer to them from this point on as Ohio Boy and Ohio Girl.

When you meet people on a drunken night, or on a party circuit, or while out of town, how often do you exchange information and follow up? We did. Unusual, yes, but we had a common ground. That place. That favorite thing in the world. She and I talked on the phone many times, many nights. We talked about her on-again, off-again boyfriend, my on-again, off-again boyfriend, about school, about work, about life.

Usually, the calls lasted an hour and a half, and I was paying dearly on my phone bill for this burgeoning friendship. Calls were really expensive back then. Even when she called me, I called right back. She was still a student. I had a full-time job.

Anyway, one of their three fell by the wayside, Ohio Boy. He finally felt courageous enough to come out as gay and changed his lifestyle and friends in some way that split he and the others apart. But the rest of us went on strongly.

Not one month after meeting for the new year celebration, she drove from Ohio to Indy's house and then he drove to my house in St. Louis. I felt so validated, so wonderful, that they came out. They stayed for a three-day weekend. I showed them around town. We listened to music, watched videos, drank a little, made the worst video you have ever seen. The video really sucked balls.

We made plans for February to go on a short, overnight road trip. We met in mid-Illinois to collect together in one car and make the trek to this spot. I guess I need to explain something here. At this place, there was an inner circle that was extremely popular, hard to get to know.

There was an outer circle of people who I knew very well, having developed a rapport with them over a period of years. It was always clear to me that one of their pet peeves was for strangers to figure out they knew the power-hitters and ask to meet them. Talk about insincerity. I never did ask. Not time after time, not year after year of going there.

One reason was that the friends I'd made, I didn't consider them *contacts* or *stepping stones* to the rich, powerful inner circle of people. I considered them friends.

Truth be told, there really was another reason, a bigger reason. The reason I liked this place so much was its leveling factor. In reality, I was a bit of a nerd, a geek, a dork, a slender midwestern poet. I actually *liked* the distance, the remoteness of it all, a lot.

When I went there... to the inner circle, I was this mystery person who sometimes showed up and then quietly disappeared again into the night. The place was crawling with gold-diggers, wannabes, groupies, and whores. In fact, the reason I had designed that historically-significant, artsy shirt was that I never wanted to be mistaken for one of those people.

Ohio Girl, Indy and I went on a road trip to our place. Our *Sedona* if you will. They were short of cash, again, so they provided gas money to meet up with me, and from there, I provided the vehicle, gas money, food money, hotel money, and all other expenses. Hey, they were my friends, right?

Night Number One

We arrived at our destination. Upon stopping in and greeting my outer circle that morning to let them know I was in town, I saw the inner circle surprisingly there in daylight. It's not like they were vampires. It's just that I wasn't usually there in the daytime and the events were always at night.

The four of them were at a distant side of the room. It freaked me out because, on the trip, it turned out that those people were the only topic holding Ohio Girl's interest. I already had this vague feeling of apprehension. Even worse, my two closest outer circle friends were falling over themselves immediately to meet the girl with the Neve Campbell mystique, this pre-Emo, underground beauty, and I was their inside connection.

We did leave and went out about the town, took naps, ate, and got ready for our night. I slipped into a black turtleneck and jeans, topping the turtleneck with my art design original that had earned accolades and acclaim. It's how the inner circle knew I was there on any given night, from my safe distance of blurred dorkiness.

Ohio Girl, she looked at me and said, "You're not going to wear that shirt, are you? You look like a dork." I was rather taken aback. She had no comprehension of its meaning, its Picasso-like attraction. I sound so elitist. Heh. I didn't know what to do.

Then she added the all-too-perfect "Look, I'm just telling you this as a friend because I care about you." The iconic shirt came off and for the first time, I wore something chosen by someone else and it looked bad, in my humble opinion, and was just not me at all.

The night actually went well until the last moments. You turn one wrong corner, switch locales to wind down, find one, completely-dead hotel bar to simply discuss the night before heading home, and boom… in walks Victim Number One, hereby referred to as Single Guy of the Inner Circle. To his defense, he was the only single one and was obviously taken with Ohio Girl. He asked to join our table.

I motioned to an empty seat and said, "Of course, c'mon." Then, we talked, really casually and comfortably. She watched us talk, but offered nothing, even as he tried to warm her to him with kindness, eye contact, smiles of interest. And then, he asked for us to come back the next night. He personally invited us. To our special place. I told him it was tempting, but we had such a long drive, in different directions to get back home. He said he would watch for us just in case.

Argument number one broke out back at our hotel. Ohio Girl said we just had to stay, and I was driving, and if we left it would ruin Indy's and her lives. I told her I had to work. Indy chimed in and offered the thought that he was willing to lose *his* job over an opportunity like this. It might never happen again.

I looked at them. No money, willing to lose it all, everything hinging on me. Of course, I chose friendship over logic.

Night Number Two

Night number two proved he really did watch for us to show. For the first time, the outer circle had been apprised of our potential arrival and were on the lookout for us. We were met with free drinks, VIP treatment and later escorted to a private chat area.

That sounds weird, but basically, there was a room away from the noise. It was fully lit, nothing sleazoid, no drugs being doled out. We sat there and talked for an hour or so. Well, not all of us. Single Guy was joined by Victim Number Two, hereby referred to as Married Guy. He was a newly remarried man who was brimming with joy, talking about his family life and the pending arrival of a new baby boy.

The discussion was actually quite pleasant. I was surprised by my level of complete comfort with these two and chuckled at my earlier fears of being too nerdy. They didn't treat me like I was a dork at all. They treated me with graciousness, kindness and as their equal. Most of the discussion was directed toward me, as neither she nor Indy really spoke up.

She did manage to say, "Give me a light!" And, she muttered, "I hate that kind of beer. It sucks." Other than being confused by those lines, I remember nothing of verbal content from her. To my dismay, Single Guy tried again with her by suggesting we alter our plan, well, my plan to hold down a job. He asked us to come back again the next night. Both of my friends immediately agreed, while I swallowed hard at the growing severity of my situation and the apprehension grew.

Argument number two broke out at a truck-stop diner that had private jukeboxes at each table.

"The night had gone better than ever expected. How could we stop now? We were *in*." I don't know if I was psychic or just being negative, but I saw this all blowing up in my face. And, I was out of money. I would have to hit the ATM and maybe even do a credit card advance payment. I was not only out of planned money, I had spent my emergency fund hidden in a key box in my engine. I was now faced with retrieving bill money and running short for the month.

Tears slid down my cheeks as I pleaded to go home and come back another time. But no. "If we were *in* now, it could be short-lived. We needed to ensure it." It's like they couldn't see me crying, like I was a million miles away. I don't know.

I didn't want to ensure anything. But, again, I still believe to this day that friendship is worth more than any job. Had it been a career, maybe that would have been different. It was just a job.

Yeah, we stayed for a third night. I spent more money on food for all, we watched videos, window shopped, etc.

Night Number Three

The place that night was so packed, there was no room to be a VIP. We just enjoyed the moments alone, knowing that what was to come was to be more special. We went back to our hotel, where a van was waiting for us.

My outer circle buddy, Billy, loaded us into it and we were driven to a little corner bar that was quiet and nearly empty. There were, like, two patrons, and then the rest of the people we knew. These guys had chosen a place which was leveling to them. No one there thought or knew they were rich, powerful, or important. Ironic, really.

It was then she pulled me aside into an empty bathroom. Not the first crack in her veneer, but the first telling one to me. She said, "The reason I've barely said anything to these guys is that I'm so intimidated. And, what makes it worse is… you're not. You're completely comfortable talking about any subject, and I have no idea what to say. I blurted out I hate that beer and give me a light because I was struggling. If you're really my friend, do me this favor. If Married Guy talks to me, just walk away. Please."

I said, "I've taken two extra days off work, probably lost my job, spent my planned money, my emergency money, my bill money, driven us a thousand miles the wrong direction and you're telling me *not* to talk to this guy if I get the chance, because I treat him normally and we have a rapport? Are you serious?"

She said, "If you're my friend, you'll walk away. It's the only way I'll be comfortable being myself."

We left the bathroom and went into the main bar. Married Guy was there and greeted me with a huge, warm hug and smile. He hugged Ohio Girl, also, though she didn't receive it well and looked really awkward.

I said, "It's so good to see you, um, I have to go over there though. Take care." He looked really, super confused, as perplexed as a face can get and leaned over and kissed me in a sweet way that didn't even scare the bejesus out of me. He said he was on his way out anyway. His wife was potentially going into labor, and he was actually staying in our hotel because he'd moved too far away to drive home on weekends.

He pointed out Single Guy and asked me to go cheer him up. Single Guy was drunk, was really down, and would be glad to talk to me. I told Married Guy how excited I was for him and his wife, how happy to have seen him before he left, (and to his confused face) hugged him goodbye. He gave me a cheek kiss and looked like he knew something was up. I walked away, as previously asked, leaving Ohio Girl alone with Married Guy.

I walked over to Single Guy and sat down. He perked up from his doom-and-gloom mood and we had a great conversation, for about two minutes. She came over, looking defeated, angry, pouting for a moment, then her face lit up with some clever idea and she turned her sights towards the single guy of the inner circle.

After rubbing his thigh and flirting immensely, she needed to use the ladies' room. She needed me to come with. Needed. I was getting the look. In the empty bathroom, she told me something that knocked me flat.

"Look, Married Guy left the building, and he married a slut and she's having his baby, but I'm his soul mate. I've been in love with him for years. That's why I can't talk around him. I can't take it. This guy is my only chance. He's single. If I get *in* with him, I'll be able to get closer to Married Guy. He'll see that I'm the one for him. I'll never get closer to Single Guy if he keeps talking to *you*. Why is it so easy for you to talk to anyone about anything? Walk away. Let me have my chance."

Oh, yes. Yes, she did.

I was stunned. I countered with logic, of course. "You don't even know this guy you say you love. You just met him last night. If you don't know him, it can't be love. Maybe you have a crush, infatuation, adoration, I don't know. What I do know is he just remarried and he's so obviously happy. He's beaming! If you *love* him, then you need to trust his judgment. Let him alone. And, furthermore, to use Single Guy as a vehicle to reach Married Guy is beyond immoral and unbelievably unethical on every level. I care about them, whether I know them well or not. I won't let you do that."

Her face set with determination and she looked straight into my eyes. "Oh, sweetie, you're not going to stop me."

And she was right…

I was so disgusted with her behavior, I walked back to Single Guy, told him goodnight, and thanked him for his generosity. I think he'd bought a round or something. I got another confused look but endured it. Then, I walked to the other room where the bar was and was sucker punched by something I never saw coming.

There's something I haven't told you. Because it's embarrassing. Within that inner circle of four, there was one guy who did intimidate me. In this story, he will be referred to as Mentor Guy. Because he was my mentor guy, my Mr. Miagi if you will. I never told him, and he'd never have guessed and probably not cared either. He was underestimated by nearly everyone, unbelievably astute, yet wore a zany façade that fooled most into seeing him as just a caricature. Around him, I could not speak. I had been told by a mutual friend that he didn't suffer fools gladly and that freaked me out and put me at a loss for words. He was a mentor of mine without knowing it, cultured yet down to earth. He had a steady upbringing and was a true family man with integrity, warmth, and compassion. He had somehow turned zany into cool.

I walked to the main bar and ordered a beer and uncannily… up walked Mentor

Guy to the other end of the same bar. He eyed me in a new evaluation. There I was, after hours, in his personal space. He looked at the beer in my hand, squinted, and I received the coldest stare I'd ever received in my life. Nothing hurts like a silent stare. It had come from the one person I was afraid wouldn't like me, the one man I didn't want to ever know I was just a geeky nerd out on the town, trying to erase a stigma of shame and feel a sense of belonging.

Mentor Guy was displeased. That mystery girl in the artsy shirt had invaded personal space and, ironically, had been mistaken for one of the shallow, gold-digging groupies that always fluttered around. I was so crushed by that icy stare I had no words. I felt like I'd just been crucified and died a thousand deaths. So, I set down my full beer and walked away from the whole situation.

If you are the company you keep, it was time for me to change company. Right? Ohio Girl and her need for being *in* had pulled me into a part of a nightlife that I was grossly unequipped to handle. I thought I'd take the high road and went back to the hotel.

Thinking it was a brilliant idea, I drank a beer. And then, a second and third beer... that might have happened, too. Yay me. I have no idea how much time passed… an hour, three, I don't know. I was just upset. I felt dirty or something.

She came back to the hotel room, and just when I thought it couldn't get any worse, she said, "Oh, hon, I just don't know what to do. The wrong guy likes me. He thinks I want him, and he gave me the key to his hotel room." She held it up.

"But I only like him as a friend. I went to the other hotel room, the guy I like. The door was open and there's a group there just sitting around to see if his slut wife goes into labor. Anyway, I told him that his buddy likes me and wants me. And I told him I just can't do that, because you have a huge crush on Single Guy. I told him that you've liked him for years and I know it would never work out because he's a partier and you're just an innocent sweetheart from the Midwest, but because he's so well-traveled and rich, and powerful, and you're a bit star-struck and a little obsessed with him.

I stared at her. "You said *what*????"

"Of course, I told him you weren't dangerous, and they had no reason to worry. It's just that you had built your life around the times you got to come here and see this guy in the room, from a distance."

I said, "But, you know the guy I've dated a guy on and off for the last year and a half… We've given each other advice on dating. You know who I like, like *that*. Why would you make up I liked Single Guy?" She continued...

"Well, Married Guy was really shocked. He said he said he had no idea you had a thing for Single Guy, and that you always had acted so normal. He never would have guessed that. Then, I told him that I just wanted to be a good friend to you. How could I date a guy you liked and still be a good friend? Well, he was so comforting. He told me that there was nothing I could do and that it was so sweet of me to be so considerate of you, but I needed to follow my heart."

I tossed in, "Did you happen to tell him that you were just trying to impress him to get him to leave his pregnant wife and the single guy, who was depressed, was just a disposable pawn in your messed-up little scheme?"

She laughed, then talked softly again. "Of course not. Oh, sweetie, you know how much you like this guy."

"I do?"

"Oh, it's so obvious. And I don't want to hurt you…. But then, I went to Single Guy and told him…"

"You whaaa…"

"He's really angry right now. I mean he is super pissed off. He just didn't see it coming either. He said you've never flirted at all. Completely platonic. He had no idea! Now, he is mad, really mad that he can't be with me because of you. He even said he'd fuck you if that would mean he could fuck me…"

Oh, yes, she did.

Tears came hard. What a low blow.

I have no idea if he ever said that. He probably did. He was drunk and mad at her sudden story that made me a scapegoat after her heavy flirting. When I finally could speak, I said with a clear understanding...

"You just ruined my reputation. They think the impression they got over years of knowing me was wrong and they've been told privately by someone in-the-know that I'm some obsessed, crazy, small-town, doe-eyed dreamer, trying to move up in the glamorous world and I'm starstruck by some powerful guy who can take me places. Yeah, of course they didn't see that coming based on how I acted because you made it up. Which means all the trust I'd earned is gone. It's all gone."

She smiled so sweetly, so believably my good friend. And, she said, in the kindest, most syrupy-sweet voice, "I told you that you weren't going to stop me."

I was way too drunk, way too hurt, way too stunned and blubbering in tears. I left and went to my friend Billy's room. I told him what happened, and he was infuriated.

He said, "I've known these guys for years. They meet women like her all the time. *Trust* me, they will never believe that load of crap. It's obvious who is who and what is what. Don't even worry for a second. They would never believe that conniving, psycho bitch!"

A little later, he went down the hall for ice and his phone rang. I thought he might be calling from the front desk or something with a question. I answered his phone. It was her target, Married Guy, looking for Billy.

He recognized my voice and said, "Hey, Sweetie, while I have you on the phone, I know you don't want to hear this right now. But just listen. Single Guy is not the right guy for you. You may think you're in love with him, sweetheart, but you don't even know him. I know how easy it can be to get obsessed with someone, but I promise you… you are wonderful, and you will meet the right guy. It's not him."

I said, "But, that's not…" and he said, "Tell Billy I called. I have to keep this line open, hon." And he was gone.

Never believe her? Never fall for that? Well, at least Married Guy was nice.

He's one of the most gracious human beings on the planet, but time told the story…

Four Months Later

Yes, let's cut to four months later… She invited me out to make up for her behavior and talk to me. She asked me to buy tickets to an event and meet her there. Then, when Single Guy found out I was coming and was afraid 'because I was obsessed with him', she ditched me and left me alone in the arena with two tickets.

Ironically, Married Guy, her *man*, saw me, hugged me, and brought me back to the group. He introduced me to his older son, who was seven at the time, and sat me with his family. She was sitting there looking visibly upset. Interesting. I smiled inside. I saw pain in her face and this dark part of me got pleasure from it. Then, it was time to go and I got hugs, kisses, and goodbyes from Married Guy. I was left with her. She broke into tears. It was quite the highlight, actually.

She said that everything had gone wrong and, for some reason, Single Guy *thought* she liked Married Guy and was not speaking to her… simply because she had put a pillow on Married Guy's lap and laid down on it and Single Guy walked in and stormed out. Poor Married Guy was left to explain her behavior to his seven-year-old boy. Ugh.

Anyway, it was so nice to see her behavior blow up in her face. In the sweetest, most sincere voice I could fake, and with a straight face, I said, "Tell me everything."

She did, and I suppressed the smiles and cheers of her being recognized for the shallow, two-faced, lying scumbag scheming bitch that she so was. Then, I almost lost it and laughed out loud when she asked me,(I kid you not!) if I could fix it all for her, because I was so trusted and had known them for years.

I shook my head as I said, "But, oh sweetie, did you forget? You destroyed my reputation. Reputation is a fragile thing. There's nothing I can do to help you now. I'm so sorry." She cried some more. My inner me smiled so big. Isn't that awful?

You know, I thought, for me then, it could be good again. But it was too late. Even though they found her out, they still had no reason to believe she had lied about me. Her plan had been masterful, I'll give her that. They understood that she was shallow and playing them against each other. They didn't know that I was not obsessed nor trying to hook up with the single guy or any of them at all.

I went back a few times. Single Guy, he avoided me. Married Guy was warier around me and Mentor Guy, the one I admired the most, became the caricature he was known to be once again. I believe that

Number Four in the group remained uninvolved and unaware of the situation in its entirety, so let's call him Oblivious Guy this once.

For what it's worth, I had been demoted. Of course, I ended my pretend friendship with her: Ohio Girl. I realized that there had been so many signs of her insincerity along the way. I hadn't wanted to see them, because I'd never been befriended by a gorgeous, trophy friend. In truth, it had made me feel important, which was my most shallow moment to date. And, I had paid dearly for being so shallow.

Yes, I learned a lesson, but at a cost greater than anything but death. Remember, that place was my favorite place in the world. It was my escape from stress, from work, from being a dorky bookworm girl next door. It was my favorite thing to do and it had been tainted.

I no longer blended in and became an equal. Now and forever, I stood out and had become an outsider. It was not the most painful hardship of my life, but it was the hardest lesson I ever had to endure. I should have known better.

There are some things you can never undo, some places you can never un-visit, some types of innocence that can never be regained, some impressions that can never be rectified. Sure, I could have told those guys, "She made that up." But she was so believable I nearly wondered if I had a crush on that guy when I was head over heels for my back-home dude. It's more likely they would have thought I was so humiliated I was downplaying some crush to save face.

I could have said that I was skittish around guys, a violent trauma survivor, and had they even mildly flirted they would have seen me shy away in terror, not blossom under the affection. I did consider it. Sure.

To clarify what had really happened would have been to vulnerably disclose that I was awkward and socially inept and had escaped into the crowds to feel a sense of hard-to-find safety and a sense of belonging in that one special, irreplaceable spot. It would have been admitting to things I never wanted them or anyone to know.

To leave it be, I was viewed as an obsessed Midwestern girl trying to live out some kind of big-city fantasy. Maybe, I even looked like a starstruck groupie looking for a hot time with, I don't know... the chosen ones, so to speak. One of the fan club.

I chose what, at the time, felt like the lesser of two evils. I might not make the same choice today, but back then, I actively decided that I'd much rather have that inner circle of guys mistake me for some kind of crushing wannabe than to be crystal clear about who or what I really was.

I walked away for good, from my favorite thing in the world, my favorite place in the world. Forever. It was like... I'd gone to the dark side that night and would wear the Scarlet Letter forever. It was my own fault, too. I'm not blaming anyone but me. Let me be clear.

Everything was exactly perfect until I changed it. I had the perfect escape, the perfect place, the best moments ever. Yet, I allowed myself to be bullied and much worse… to be shallow. If I lived my life over, when that moment arose again, I would never have run the risk of falling for her schemes or crossed that line.

There's a verse that's in a song from 2005 that I can't print here without having the money and permission, and I have neither. It expresses how I feel about that moment, back in time. It was a beautiful memory, a lesson learned, a betrayal that stole a piece of my heart, a favorite place that shifted from refuge to refuse.

As I look at the photo albums of those days and see her photograph, here is where I would place that stanza. I'd say... I miss that place and those faces I can't erase or replace it. I miss it right this second, which is hard to believe. It was so hard to stay and too hard to leave.

You know, if I could go back to that pivotal moment, I wouldn't be shallow. I wouldn't cross the line. That distance that I had, that I loved, it would have remained. And, I *never* would have lost my favorite thing.

The truth is: sometimes, you lose.

Another Sad Day in Paradise

The words you said – they threw me
For a loop, I guess they say.
It made me really angry
That you'd think of me that way.

I picked up all my anger
Cast it aside with words
And found that anger really
Just covered up a hurt.

I didn't understand
If I was hurt by seeing truth
Or because I wasn't shallow
And thought, perhaps, you knew.

Now, you have unleashed a pain
No one would want to see.
Pain should be kept hidden
Only happy thoughts set free.

While I was left cut open
By words not meant to hurt
I ran the gamut of emotion
A simple phrase had come and stirred.

The sadness got sobbed out, so I
Looked deeply underneath
Then cried when I saw what was there
I never liked to see.

The pain came reeling through my head
And tore apart my mind.
Scabs that covered unhealed wounds
Dripped blood and tears and wine.

When the tears had run their course
Just emptiness remained
A vision of the scars and
Quilted remnants of the pain.

My old mind, it remembered
An old truth I'd once discovered
The baggage in my heart
Would be too much for any other.

You see, I'd never ask for empathy
For pity or compassion.
The Law of Threefold's always just
I made this baggage happen.

The weight I carry doesn't hail
From some traumatic life event
But from the secrets and the shame
And base embarrassment.

The funny thing, you needn't fear
What worried you the most.
The one thing that is crystal clear
I'm haunted by my ghost.

How many times can I endure
A cathartic, soul release
And have blackness seeping back across
My heart and mind with ease?

If I could check this baggage
All the way to Timbuktu
And never go and claim it
That's what I'd like to do.

But on my back, it's carried
The weight presses on my soul
The only thing alive in me
Are the words to let you know.

A Match Made in Heaven

[18+ Trigger Warnings]

I'm married to the most wonderful woman in the world, the perfect match for me, however unlikely. How that came to pass is a story I've never shared with anyone, until now.

****

The year was 1991. I was twenty-three and living in a small city in Anytown, USA. Still single and living with a roommate I'd known since college.

Janet was a great girl, but a real homebody. The few times I convinced her to go out with us, she'd sit alone at the table as we all danced and partied. She wasn't extremely large, but the bars were crowded with Playmate wannabes, and she just didn't compare. I know it must have hurt, and I know that's why she begged off of most occasions. The show she just had to see or the book she had to finish were only a guise for the pain she didn't want to endure. Again.

I was tall, dark and handsome by society's standards. Janet took all of my incoming messages with a smile and would pass them to me each night as I came home, usually over her bowl of ice cream.

It was Saturday night. Janet stayed home again. I went out to a new club to meet friends who would be showing up. The bar was already smoky at 10:30. The lights were dim and the music on the dance floor was insanely loud. Sitting at the bar, waiting for my buddies, was quieter, almost tolerable.

I talked up a tall, pretty blonde who was sitting alone beside me. My mind felt amusement as I thought about the ironies of life. Janet sat home because she was too plain to be asked out and this woman sat alone in a bar because men were too threatened by rejection.

She said her name was Lisa. Two hours later my friends still hadn't shown. I felt a bit woozy. The lights were really bothering me, and the noise seemed almost surreal. Lisa and I walked out together. She noticed I didn't look so well and offered to drive me home. I declined. Then I stumbled.

She said, "Please. Come to my house. You can stay on the couch. My best friend was killed by a drunk driver. Please don't insist on driving."

The truth is, I didn't feel drunk. But her words were so strong, so wrought with emotion. Responsibly, I accepted her help. I can barely remember stumbling into her house. But I do remember coming to.

The bedroom was dimly lit, slightly smoky, and smelled like cheap incense. A bathroom across the room glowed from a night light. A dressing table was to my left. On the table, a long blond wig was perched on a wig stand. I winced. Then I heard a voice: a harsh, gruff, mocking voice.

"Looks like Mr. Perfect is waking up."

I turned my head to the right and saw a huge hand come at my face. The room darkened. I realized I'd just been blindfolded. That was the first time I tried to move. I couldn't.

My hands were bound by rope above my head. My ankles were restrained together.

Her voice said, "Maybe, he needs a little more."

"All right, Lisa, but not too much. We want him conscious."

A teaspoon of something snaked down my throat. I remembered how to scream just as the gag was pushed into my mouth and tied around my head.

I felt woozy again. The room felt like it was moving. Too late, I realized that I was. My body hit the floor with a thud. I couldn't fight. I couldn't move. What happened next lasted hours. It was gruesome, vile and inhuman. I wrote it all out, right here. Then, I realized it's too much to share. You don't really want to know. I don't really want to say. I hit the backspace key and removed it.

What you need to know is it was violent beyond your imagination. It was twisted and dark and involved all three of us, two unwilling. I'm not sure why she followed his instructions, why she allowed him to abuse me, abuse her, do things that were unspeakable to both of us, why she let him make her his accomplice. When he did turn his attention from myself to her, I remember feeling relieved that I was no longer the focus and horrified at the sounds that came through my blindfold. As I said, it lasted for hours. It was physically excruciating. It was emotionally disturbing. I'd never been tormented, mocked, tossed around like a ragdoll, intimidated. Eventually, everything comes to an end. I don't remember that. I remember chaos., and then silence. Everything was dark and quiet.

****

Light began to stir me to consciousness. My eyes slowly opened. I was sitting in the driver's seat of my car. I looked around, through the windows. Bells rang out. I stared. I was in a church parking lot. Services were just beginning. I slowly raised my hand to adjust the rear-view mirror. My right wrist had rope burns. I winced. I gingerly moved my arm and turned the mirror to my face. I had abrasions over most of it.

I realized what had happened to me and the vomit couldn't stay down. I reached for the door handle, then couldn't bring myself to throw up on church grounds. The indecision brought it up all over me before I could turn towards the passenger seat. After heaving up what was left in my system over my clothes, the car seat, the steering wheel, I sat and stared for several minutes.

Finally, I rolled down the window and started my car. And not knowing what else to do, I drove home. It was mid-morning when I stumbled incoherently into the house. Janet heard me. She came out of her room in an oversized t-shirt and stopped in her tracks. Our eyes met. She beckoned me with just a look.

What to do? Call the police? I knew what she was thinking. My shame was too great to contact anyone. I'd realized on the drive home that I couldn't identify either one of the people who'd attacked me. I didn't know where they lived, where I'd been. I remembered the blonde wig on the stand.

I shook my head slowly, then lowering it, I headed to the bathroom. She came with me. I turned on the faucet and began to run a bath. Her eyes were filled with tears, but she found inner strength from somewhere and began to help me undress. Every abrasion, every burn – made more tears flow from her eyes.

I stood in front of her completely naked for the first time. My body was a mess. Dried blood was caked to my skin. She helped me step into the tub, and then to my surprise, she lifted off her t-shirt with a self-conscious hesitancy. She slipped off her underwear. And she crawled in behind me, gently.

With a washrag, she began to cleanse my body. The water became pink from the blood as she soaped and rinsed my wounds. She let the water out and helped me stand. With the shower running, she soaped my hair and my body again, making sure no trace of that vile man resided on my skin. She gently dried me with her favorite, fluffy towel and then dressed my wounds one by one.

In the bedroom, she put me on her bed. Smelling mildly of her familiar perfume, she pulled the covers up and we lay there together. She never asked me to describe what happened. Not then. Not ever. I cried into her arms for the longest time. And then I slept. I'd wondered on the drive home if I'd ever sleep again. But with her there beside me, I was completely safe. After the tears, sleep came easily.

Later that day, she brought me some soup and crackers and slowly spoon-fed me small bites. She called into work for me, told them I had mono and would be out for a while. She called her work and told them the same.

Day by day, she took care of me. I regained my strength, my inner strength, slowly. Several days after the event, we were watching tv together, snuggled up on the couch. Something made me laugh. It sounded strange. I realized I hadn't laughed, hadn't even spoken, in days.

Time passed. I went back to work. Daily routine began to replace the level of guilt, shame and dread that had encompassed my life. My friends were concerned about me. They told me I just wasn't the same since getting mono. They said I never wanted to party anymore. They were right. That was a chapter of my life that had closed.

A month after the event, Janet went with me to the clinic. My results were in. They wouldn't tell me over the phone. They said that was standard procedure. I was terrified as the nurse sat down across from me. She said that the preliminary tests were negative. She looked me over closely and added, "However, if you have some reason to be concerned, you'll need to be tested again in six months to be sure."

Those six months were the longest of my life. Janet slept with me every night. And it was a comfort, but it awakened fears inside me. My body had healed. The natural response of a woman next to me could make me hurt the woman I loved most in the world. I'd surprised myself. I thought of it again. I loved this woman.

I no longer saw the awkward, heavy girl from my college days. I saw a woman of grace and beauty, a woman of generosity. I knew I never wanted to be with another woman again.

The results of the second test finally came. I was clear. Janet and I broke down. We basically cried in relief, together.

She'd never spoken of her feelings for me. I wondered just how long she'd loved me. How long had she watched me notice every woman around her, and not see what was right in front of me?

I thought to myself that night, while Janet made our favorite dinner. There was no reason to jump into a physical relationship, even though I was physically ready and emotionally healed. I knew I wanted to be with her always.

Another thought occurred to me like a jolt. Had this whole thing not happened to me, how long would I have taken to change? Would I have ended up with her? I knew now how thankful I was for the savage attack, as crazy as it seemed. And then dinner was ready.

I stepped into the bathroom first. Then I went to the table. I knelt down before her and took her hand. She gasped. Her eyes welled up.

"Janet, I don't have a ring yet, but if you'll accept this piece of dental floss from a loving, devoted man, as a token of my intentions, we can replace it with a ring of your choosing in short order." Tears gently slid down her cheeks. "Janet, will you be my wife?"

She sucked in her breath and swallowed hard. Words finally came.

"Oh, yes. Oh, yes, of course I'll marry you." Her hands slid around my neck and we held each other, there in the kitchen until long after the food had gotten cold.

The next day we shopped for a ring and two months later, we were married in a beautiful ceremony to the complete surprise of all my still-partying friends. That was nine years, two houses and three children ago. I feel the same today as I did back then.

I know that everything happens for a reason. With all the trauma that still comes back to haunt me, even today, I still know I ended up being the luckiest man in the world.

"I love you, Janet."

Shaman Eyes

I guess I'm like deep water
The surface feigning calm -
Below are currents, sight unseen
That churn within the storm.

I walk through life enlightened
(In my own sadistic mind.)
With a hidden inner turmoil
I remotely keep denying.

As different levels surface
At home and work and play
All think they could dissect me well
But none could, I can say.

There are those who know me
Who would simply say I'm smart
Blunt, direct, yes - bottom line
Without much soul or heart.

Others who have met me
Have met my inner child
Who needs support and guidance
And is questioning and mild.

There are none, I think, who know me
And all my soul denies
Until I meet a seer
A man with shaman eyes.

Who stabs me with perception
A piercing, fleeting glance
That reflects the lies I tell myself
With the sharpness of a lance.

Recovery is not easy
With truth trying to sneak in
How much time it takes to
Live in all my lies again.

Words Strike Back

The words resented being used and abused over and over. The man was always grabbing them and slinging them at people.

The angry words didn't mind so much. They never felt like they were used enough. "Screw you buddy" and "up yours" were happy to comply.

But the sensitive words didn't like being grabbed or tossed about. They liked being caressed and nurtured.

The man came in again today. The words cowered in the corner. He found them anyway. He chose "I love you" and "I could never live without you." These were beautiful words surely, but he'd used them all too often.

He could piece phrases together quite well and the words could never truly hide from him. The individual letters were usually okay, except *I*. He liked that letter the best, used it all the time.

He continued his behavior for years: stealing words, twisting them around, putting them out there, but never the meanings behind them.

Finally, they couldn't take it any longer. They decided to press charges.

The words took their case to the high court and just cause was found with little delay.

The man was brought in against his will. He was pompous and arrogant. He thrust his finger into the face of the judge and shouted that he'd get a lawyer.

The judge told him to sit down and shut up. Flustered, he began to slew words in all directions at the top of his lungs.

The benches emptied at once as all the words looked for a place to hide from his wrath.

There wasn't any place.

At long last, he began to sling words together that didn't even exist. Security was called and the room was settled into a semblance of order.

The judge warned him that no more outbursts would be tolerated, and he was not allowed to come in here and start beating up on words left and right.

Left and *Right* were very relieved to hear this, I might add.

The proceedings began.

Slowly, words came forward to tell their tale of woe and abuse.

The judge listened, for in the high court there were no lawyers. *Anger* and *Bitterness* testified first to their abuse. Even though they like being used, he did so selfishly.

Next, *Innocence* took the stand. He stated that every time this man had been in trouble, he had pulled this word from his hat.

Guilty eagerly agreed with the testimony. He said there were many times he should have been used by this man, but never was. Entitlement got up there and said though his word was never used, the full meaning was always clear.

Against their will, *Deceit* and *Betrayal* were both called up as hostile witnesses. Begrudgingly, they told of the man's shenanigans.

The court was adjourned for a break. At 2:30, the reason was not quite clear. All the words were whispering to one another, and it was so cluttered and wispy, the man couldn't understand one word.

They could be quite clever, you know.

During the break, the man felt admirably confident. He was sure that the testimony of mere words was utter nonsense.

Who would listen to such lowly commoners?

The court came back to order and a hush fell over the room. The double doors at the back swung open.

Standing there was a group of words. He looked them over closely.

Promise, Truth, Hope, and *Justice* stood there in a line. They looked very smug.

The man's confidence buckled a little and he squirmed in his seat. He squinted and started to lift out of his chair to get a better look. Together, in line, the group walked up the long aisle to the front of the room.

As they walked, a muted sound of astonishment followed them up the aisle.

They stopped at the opening of the room. And parted.

And there in the center, was glorious *Love*. He fell back into his chair with a thud, flabbergasted. He knew he had just lost the battle.

He stood up and faced the judge. "It's true," he blurted out. "I am guilty of abusing these words, of stealing their meanings. Why it matters, I don't know, but I have used them and manipulated them, over and over, for my own sordid gains. I suppose I should feel remorse or sorry. But I don't. Those are words I've never used."

The words shook their heads with sadness at this utter truth.

The judge told him that he was guilty as charged.

Guilty was happy to finally be used.

His sentence was a lack of sentence. In other words, there would be no other words. He was forbidden to use letters, words, phrases, or sentences ever again.

I would tell you how that made him feel, but he never said.

He lived the rest of his life alone, lying to no one, deceiving no one, betraying no one.

And the words were so happy that they wanted to jump for joy. But they couldn't because *Joy* was on vacation in the Bahamas.

So, they settled for sighing with *Relief*.

Too Close to The Sun

I was in the dark,
in the cold, afraid of the light.

Afraid it would scar me,
my eyes, my skin.

But inside, I began to suffocate.
The sun was so kind, warm, and inviting.
I had been missing this my entire life.

I couldn't walk away.
I couldn't go back in.

I knew I would start to sizzle, eventually.
I knew I needed water, or I wouldn't last.

But I was too attached to escape.
All I could do was stand there and enjoy it
Enjoy my pending disintegration and death

And let it happen in its own time.
Maybe, I should have been sad
to find out I was mortal.

But his love was more welcoming
than any I'd ever had.

I got too close to the sun,
but he was worth it.

Call Me Crazy

Okay, I'm a little different. But it's not like I have cornered the market on crazy or anything. I've just chosen a path no one else seems to have taken. You know all about the road less traveled, right? Well, at some point, I don't remember exactly when. I came to a crossroads.

The left side was the well-worn path taken by most people. It's the one I had been on before I came to the crossroads. I knew I didn't belong there because people looked at me like I was too different, too abnormal. Thought provoking and rebellious, I didn't fit there. I didn't look back.

I turned and started down the right side, thinking I'd meet fellow bohemians –

people who looked at life differently. And I did, but I soon found they looked at me differently. I was not different enough, not abnormal enough, not rebellious enough. I looked too much like the people on the other path, too mainstream, and I was ignored.

I came back to the crossroads and sat for a while. I didn't want to buy into keeping up with the Joneses, the commercialism, the status quo. I didn't want to dye my hair pink, or get a nose ring, or say "groovy" all the time. I sat and thought. After a time, I stood up and walked into the woods. There was no path at all. It was the wild land in between the two, never tamed.

I've been exploring in the woods now for years. I thought maybe there would be more people who didn't like either path, others who were adventurers and wanted to make their own way, without the labels found in the other two. I was wrong.

I stop in the woods now and then and watch the sunrise, and revel in it. I feel the warm wind in my face, and I inhale it. I slip down into the water of each beautiful lake I pass, and I bask in it. I build a fire at night and sing haunting, folksy songs. Sometimes I hear a flute playing, but I don't know the source of the beautiful music.

In my backpack I carry a few books. I carry a sketch pad, pencils, pens, and a notebook. When I need to rest, I sit down in the warm sunlight and I read, or I write.

I keep thinking I'll hear footsteps meandering through the foothills, but I hear none. I wait for company, someone with whom to share my thoughts and words, someone to listen to, but no one shows. I know if I change, there are many people who would accept me, back on those two paths. All I have to do is change.

But I stay in the woods, admiring the beauty and gift that's called life. I hear laughter in the stars, but I realize it's only

The Little Prince, and he's so far away. I hear the flute play and let the music soothe me. And I let the sunshine warm me. And I keep writing.

I never give up hope, because then I'd be just like them. I'm creating a new path, one without judgment or labels, no rules to belong, no membership cards. Maybe someone will follow it, and someday they'll find me. Until then, I'll remain alone, in the wild, just off the beaten path. Call me crazy . . . but maybe someday you'll join me.

Need to Be Alone

Years went by.
We worked together for a long time.
One script after another, co-written.
Drama, action, comedy, romance,
sex scenes. It didn't matter.
We could talk about anything.

Sometimes people talked.
What were we doing together?
Were we an item?
Why would he settle for me?

He would laugh, shrug it off, roll his eyes.
Put his arm around me and reassure them
We were just friends, and then, you know
I'd get a headache… One of the bad ones.
I needed to be alone.

Years went by.
Relationships came and went for both of us
More writing, well written, completed.

I'd write a funny line as he stood over me
Hands on my shoulders, reading, laughing
His pheromones could blanket a city block.

I'd be happy he was happy.
Writing my best.
Then he'd add his brilliance.
Making me warm and fuzzy.

He'd hug me like the best friend
I knew I was.
Like the best friend I always knew
That I would always be.

I had to excuse myself again.
Sensitive to light and sound, you know.
Another migraine arose from nowhere.
I needed to be alone.

Years went by.
We got old, a little wrinkled, a little worn
I'd been a sister to a lover, for a lifetime.
He had no idea about it, because
he never could see me that way.

He was, you know, simply beautiful.
I had been, at my best, simply plain.
I found him in his recliner.
A scrapbook on his lap.
He was no longer breathing.
Peaceful, life had slipped away.

The scrapbook was filled with a lifetime
Of pictures… of him loving me.
There I was, page after page:
Writing, sleeping, laughing, smiling.

How did I not see him seeing me?
For all these years, all these decades?
The truth is I was never alone.
Until now.

Lightning Strikes

The lightning struck the tree with an ear-splitting force. I wasn't around when the tree fell, but I know it made a deafening sound. It had been the tree I climbed as a little girl, a tree my father had climbed when the farm was his. I didn't think anything could destroy it. I didn't think it could become part of a trail of destruction.

I had gone shopping with my husband, to lunch, then to a matinee. We knew a storm was coming, but nothing of any magnitude – or so we thought. We live out of town, so small you can barely call it a town, but it had an old theater, some quaint shops and one nice restaurant.

After forty minutes of driving back into the boonies, it was nearly dark. Almost six o'clock. As we pulled down the long drive and rounded the curve, we both looked at the charred remains of a house, still smoldering. We just sat and stared, unthinking, unfeeling.

I heard the car door open and realized my husband was walking through the deep snow, so far still from the house it hadn't melted. It must have been ten degrees by then. The wind chill was more than thirty below. I slowly regained use of my muscles and opened the car door to a harsh, bitter unwelcome.

The light remaining from the setting sun coupled with the climbing full moon illuminated a hideous sight. I held my arms tightly to my body and trudged through the snow until it became melted streams of black.

I heard the sounds of crackling here and there as I approached. My husband had made a full circle around the foundation, stepping over the fallen tree that was lying on what used to be our bedroom.

He came up and stood beside me but didn't speak. We both just stared in dismay. Finally walking away, he trudged over to the car.

I didn't know it then, but he had gone to use his cell phone. He called the volunteer fire department in Derry, the town we'd been in all day. They told him the roads were too treacherous to get here with any speed, especially as darkness was falling rapidly. There was not really much of a point anyway. Not anymore.

We waited in the car with the heater running. In silence. The first sound to break the silence was the siren of a truck in the distance. It grew louder, until it was deafening. I realized, then, there was more than one siren. That didn't matter either.

The trucks pulled up and somehow found water to spray at the remains of a lifetime. I didn't really notice how they did it. My husband was out of the car, but I stayed behind, lifeless.

I don't know how long it was before he came back. He put the car into gear, and slowly backed down the driveway. I saw, then, that the firemen had turned off their lights and were leaving.

Other cars were pulling away, too. I didn't remember that any had arrived, but you know how the siren of a fire truck brings out curious onlookers.

Somehow, he got me into a hotel room. I don't know where. He helped undress me and put me in the bed. The last thing I remember was the sound of the shower running.

The next morning, I awoke with a start as the clock radio belted out monstrous music. My husband pulled the cord right out of the wall and fell back asleep. I awoke again at about ten to his gentle nudging.

He had doughnuts and coffee on the table. When had he left the room? I hadn't eaten since yesterday afternoon, but I couldn't seem to find my appetite.

We walked outside, fighting the wind all the way to the car. The weather had gotten even colder. The thunderstorm had gone, but a front had moved in. Even in the daylight, it was below zero. The wind chill hovered around twenty below. We drove back to the house and arrived there by noon.

I'd been hoping that everything had been a bad dream: too many burritos, too much drink. But we hadn't eaten burritos, we'd eaten pasta. Neither of us drank. Rounding the curve, the house again came into view. It no longer was a house, just a shambles of a foundation. Few boards stood anywhere to create a semblance of structure.

We peered at the rubble in the cold, looking for anything that was recognizable.

I couldn't tell where my Christmas tree had been. I wasn't even quite sure where the living room had been.

I knew that people would be coming by to offer encouragement at some point. They'd all expect our homeowner's insurance to cover this mess. The truth that they wouldn't know, is that we'd canceled the homeowner's insurance when the farm was taking a beating, about five years ago. We had never been able to renew it.

As I walked the perimeter of the place, I was suddenly dumbstruck. How I didn't think of it more clearly last night, I couldn't say. All I can say in my defense is I'd been in shock and registered everything before me as a complete and utter loss. But, our dog, Bartleby. Where was he? Had he gotten trapped in the blaze? We certainly did not make him stay outside in this weather.

Frozen to the bone, moving slowly in the icy air, I circled to where there used to be a back door. And steps to the basement. The steps were still there. I looked down into the inky blackness and saw water. The fire trucks...

I walked back to the car with a more determined pace and grabbed the flashlight from the glove compartment. Circling back around, my husband gave me a worried look from thirty yards away. He saw me start down those stairs.

The look of horror that crossed his face did not deter me. I continued into the darkness. The stairs held and I made my way into the basement. My feet crunched through a thin layer of ice as I came off the last step. Cold, then, just numb.

Daylight beamed down from the opening and I could see the family room dimly. Old furniture sat in three inches of water. The photographs I was going to put in an album sat in a water-soaked box on the floor. Some pictures had floated out and were stuck, along with a shoe, having floated until caught by the forming ice.

I turned around the corner and went into the laundry room. Darkness. My flashlight showed a few boards had fallen from the ceiling, but it looked safe to keep moving. I shined the light up and down and over the room. And that's when I saw it. My heart winced in pain.

Bartleby's tail was there, sticking out of a pile of cold, dirty laundry on a low sorting table. I waded across the room, breaking the layer of ice as I went, and knelt down into the water. His body was, thankfully, out of the water, his head nuzzled into some towels.

I ripped off my gloves and felt his body. Was I crazy or did I feel a bit of warmth? Was that a faint heartbeat? I moved all the clothes away from his face. His eyes were closed, but I was sure he was still alive.

I guess when he was trapped by the fire, he tried to run for safety. The doors were locked. There was nowhere to go but down. Burying himself in the clothes would have provided a filter from the water being sprayed above and from the toxic fumes of the smoke.

Some must have gotten to him, though, enough to weaken him. He would have eventually climbed up the stairs to fresh air if he'd been able to do so. I leaned down and gently lifted him into my arms, not noticing the icy water that was saturating my clothes. The light went out. Too late, I realized I'd dropped my flashlight down into the water.

I had lived in this house for thirty-five years. I figured I could find the stairs in pitch black. If nothing else, I could follow the cold draft. I bumped into a few things, and almost tripped on something floating by me. I heard a groan above my head.

I knew I'd better get out of there quickly, but I was walking through molasses. I couldn't go any faster. I turned the corner and saw the beams of daylight. The family room glowed, surreal and haunting as I turned the corner again and started up the stairs.

As I made it to the third step, my husband saw me. I could see alarm, recognition, and relief sweep across his face. I could see him thinking he'd relieve me of Bartleby and help me, but I only looked at him and said "no." He hesitated at the top, but in the end, did heed my words. Bartleby weighed seventy pounds. That was seventy more than had gone down these stairs. My husband's weight added to that would not have been a good idea. On the second step from the top, the wood bowed under my feet. I staggered and almost lost the dog, but my husband was there to steady me.

We didn't speak at all. Walking straight to the car, he opened the door for me, and I awkwardly climbed in, putting Bartleby in the back seat. I squatted down on the floorboard and stroked him. By this time, I was sure he was breathing, at least faintly. Dazed, I couldn't speak to comfort him. I could only lean my head against him and cup his head in the crook of my arm.

It was a long, bumpy ride to the veterinarian's. My husband aggressively pulled into a spot, got out and ran like a madman into the office. Moments later, he and a man in a white coat ran back with urgency. They opened the door, and the man leaned in with a stethoscope. He checked some things, then scooped the dog up and they took him inside.

On the table, under a warm light, he worked on our dog. Looking up he saw that my clothes were drenched. My jeans and sleeves were stiff from the icy water. "Why don't you go change clothes and I'll do my best to save your dog? Get a bite and come back in a few hours."

I just stared blankly at him. I was vaguely aware that I had no other clothes. He looked at me intently and raised his eyebrows.

The same thing must have occurred to him too because he flushed, then stepped out of the room for a few seconds. When he returned, he said his assistant would be back with some clothes shortly, and he laid a blanket over me.

I stared off into the distance but could feel his eyes studying me. He pulled my husband aside, by the wash basin, and talked to him in a hushed, concerned voice. I registered my husband's face. He looked surprised, anguished, then he nodded. Who knows what they were talking about?

Then, there were other men, also in white. They peered into my eyes, held my wrist, listened to my heart. I can't quite remember. By then, I was fixated by this crack in the wall across from me.

They gave me some kind of shot. I thought it was a sedative. Looking back, I realize they wouldn't have given a hypothermic woman in shock a sedative. But I didn't know. I didn't know anything. And, then I slept.

****

I woke up in a bright room. If I'd been wearing my glasses, I could have seen the details. I heard muffled voices somewhere, and then soft footsteps coming nearer. The person gasped, and I heard the footsteps take off in a run.

Then, there were people, pastel people. They lifted my wrists, and poked and prodded, and kept saying, "It's all right, sweetie, you'll be fine now. It's all right."

"Whatever," I thought distantly.

I just wanted my glasses. I wondered if I'd hit my head or been in a car accident. Maybe, they had me on really weird drugs.

I'd dreamed my house had burned down. I dreamed my dog had died in my arms.

"Bartleby."

I guess I said that aloud, because some woman's voice said, "Sweetie, everything will be fine, just fine. Don't worry now. You just work on getting better. Rest, and eat and get stronger. You could have died. Everything's going to be fine."

I slept some more. I kept hearing her voice in my dreams. During the next few days, I did get stronger. I understood where I was, in a hospital.

I understood what had happened – how the tree I'd loved and had refused to cut down had been split in two and fallen through our roof catching the power lines on the way.

Even though I now fully realized our house was gone, I knew we hadn't lost everything that mattered, just possessions. Possessions that could be replaced, with time.

Three days later, my husband pushed the wheelchair down the hallway. I'd been released. He told me the car was waiting right out front.

I could hear a crowd of people as we got closer to the lobby area. Suddenly, people applauded as I came into view. I had no idea why. I questioned my husband.

"Why are these people clapping? Since when does losing your house, or going into shock, or catching pneumonia inspire people?"

My husband smiled, that old indulgent smile that made me fall for him years ago. "Honey, it's not that. They're amazed that you had the courage to go into those ruins and that you came back with a nearly lifeless dog in your arms. The story made the local news. Then it was picked up by the national news. The donations that have come in because of it have surpassed the homeowner's insurance we used to have. Money's still coming in. Honey, the whole world's fallen in love with you."

I was stunned. "But I don't care about money, or if I made the news. I just wish I could have saved him. I wish I could have gotten there sooner – have gotten there in time. If we'd only stayed home . . ."

"If we'd stayed home, love, we'd be under that tree – dead and cooked to a crisp. It wasn't our time."

"But. I didn't want it to be his time either," I cried. He bent down, smiled, and stroked my hair. Reassuringly, he motioned over to the people with a sideways nod. Confused by that, I slowly followed his gaze.

Everyone there was smiling at me, and a hush fell over them. With an unlikely grace, they quietly parted. There, sitting behind them all, was good old Bartleby, a little thinner, wearing a homemade sign around his neck that said, "Welcome Home, Mom!"

I ran over to him, falling to my knees and hugging that big, old lug of a dog. Tears of gratitude fell down my cheeks. My husband bent down beside me and hugged us both. Bartleby licked his face, then turned to me and licked the tears off my cheek. I laughed, for the first time in days.

We were back, and back with a vengeance. That fire may have taken our house, but it would not burn up our spirit. I leaned up and kissed my husband, my arm around his neck. Cameras flashed, people cheered, applause exploded. I didn't even notice.

If I'd Met My Soulmate

If I'd met my soulmate when I was a child:

I would never have learned
my ABC's
I wouldn't have wanted
to learn how to read

I wouldn't have tried
to learn how to write
I wouldn't have learned
how to be strong and fight.

If I'd met my soulmate when I was a teen:

I would have been happy
to leisure in love
I wouldn't have pushed myself
quite far enough.

I wouldn't have tried

to earn my degree
Or find out who I am –
Just what makes me – me.

If I'd met my soulmate from twenty to
thirty:

I would have offered too little and
expected too much
I would have been self–absorbed
and a bit out of touch

I wouldn't have learned to endure
and stand tall
I wouldn't have known
you get up when you fall.

Though life has been hard
and dealt some cruel blows
I'm stronger and wiser
for all of life's lows.

I've learned to speak out

and learned to be tough
I've learned to be patient
when things seemed so rough.

I've learned to listen to stories
of people I meet
And use them as lessons,
overcoming defeat.

I've learned to be open
to more points of view
Life's not all about me,
it's about all you, too.

I've learned from mistakes
that I won't make again
I've struggled to learn
to be a good friend.

Life is a teacher
and it's taught me a lot
Life is for giving it
all that I've got.

If I'd met my soulmate, in days long ago:

I would not have been willing
to learn compromise
I would not have experience
that wizened my eyes

I just wasn't ready –
I see that now, too.
I've still so much to learn –
but I know I found you.

Caliente (NC-17)

She leaned up and turned off the water from the tap, then sank back down into the now-hot-again, bubbly water. This time, when it started to cool, she would get out and dry off.

She heard the key turn in the front door and the door open. Heavy footsteps entered and the door shut again. An acrid odor touched her nostrils. She could always smell it right away, even when he'd showered at the fire station.

She was married to someone who left every day, and he was married to a job that was dangerous. There could be a time that he didn't come home, that the doorbell would ring, and she'd open to see one of his comrades.

She dreaded the idea that he placed himself in danger, even though it was so noble, honorable, and touching.

The sounds of shoes being removed, gear being put away, keys jingling until they reached their resting place - all of these filled the steamy air. Slow, quieter footsteps came down the hallway, stopped, sensing, then proceeded to the bathroom door.

She opened the drain and stood up, grabbing the hand towel on the bar to fluff out her hair. Water started to coil down into oblivion as he stepped inside. He took the towel from her gently and scrunched it into her hair. Her body still had areas where bubbles clung to it as the water slowly drained from her skin.

His face nuzzled for a moment in her neck, kissed it, then his lips moved down to her breast, gently kissing, gently sucking, caressing the other, her skin so delicate compared to his large, calloused hand.

As he pulled back and moved his arms to her waist, the cool breeze made her nipples stand erect on her creamy soft skin.

He helped her step out of the tub so she wouldn't slip. Lowered on one knee, he kissed and nuzzled her belly, stroking it longingly with the side of his face.

She didn't know how thankful he was to have been allowed to come home to her once more. He was well aware that someday he may not be able to do so. Though he was a religious man, he didn't know what his destiny held.

Every time the sirens rang through the small town, a prayer was issued by both of them. They'd never even spoken of it, but each time he came home, smelling of fumes and smoke and death, their lovemaking was like the first time all over again.

He carried her to the bedroom as if she were a flower whose gossamer petals would come apart from the slightest breeze or touch.

Gently laying her down, he kissed so many places on her skin, softly and gently, like the famed Hawaiian waterfall of kisses.

At length, his lips found hers and she responded with an urgency so unexpected and unlike her usual gentle demeanor. Only he knew the truth of her longing, her wild side, the unhinged, unleashed woman behind the child and the lady. Only he knew of the fierce, loving animal inside this porcelain doll. He reveled in knowing this private secret, shared only by them.

He responded to her urgency with a knowing hand, drifting down her belly to the ache that was awakening and screaming for him below. There was no question how much she wanted him now, his hand slid so easily down and up and down, first like a wishbone around the area that made her back arch and arms go over her head and brace the wall.

He gently squeezed his fingers together outside, knowing less was more, and a little was all it took to make her writhe and her breathing turn to shuddered gasps and release then do it again.

He paused to let her catch her breath and its pace return to normal.

With one finger, he gently slid inside her. So small still, so fragile she was. No hurry. He curved his finger upwards and slowly stroked it against her skin, making sure to use the pad of his finger. No nails against her skin.

As she relaxed again, he slipped in two fingers, so he could slowly alternate the rhythm of his movements, all the while brushing her hair away from her face and watching the rapture and abandon take over her soul.

Her eyes were closed, her back and neck arched again, then her head swung forward with sudden force. The moment her left hand gripped the sheet, her head went back forcefully, and she gasped for breath again. Her body arched once more, shuddered uncontrollably, and her right hand pushed against the wall. It seemed her breathing came to a complete stop for at least twenty seconds as she just rode it out, shuddering, breath held, completely letting go of everything in the world.

The tactile sensation of her sliding into that abyss, the fact that his fingers could feel it, yet his mind was detached enough to observe it, amazed him. Watching her filled him with so much intensity, so much everything.

Time passed, a minute or more. She was incoherent and lost, trusting him completely. Her head lolled a little and, bit by bit, she slightly came back to reality. He kept his hand in her hair and gave her a look of awe and then he kissed her temple.

She finally moved, sighed, regained some composure, and took on the role of director. Very soft-spoken director. She found him beside her. Her arms slid around his waist, up his back and gently clung to him.

She smiled. He looked ready to explode. She'd better not prolong this encounter. She kissed him, moved one hand between them, up to his head, and with it on the back of his neck, and the other on his side - she brought him down over her.

He moved gently as he lowered himself and smiled at her with wonder. She could feel him tease her, again and again, taunting them both.

Really? At this point, she was in no shape for being made to wait. Come on. Her hands lowered to his hips, directing him a little more clearly, and her legs wrapped tightly around him. As she pushed up, they both let out of moan, the moment of penetration overcoming their senses.

They slowly rode this love together, and the ache she felt didn't go away. It grew and grew with every thrust until she thought nothing would make it release. She knew she was being very vocal.

She would stop if she could, but she couldn't. Each thrust slammed into her soul, her spirit. She whimpered, sighed, and groaned with raw pleasure, release, and abandon, and he joined her there - reckless, loving, ravenous, raw.

He pulled back and caught his breath. They moved around and around, each break offering a reprieve from climax but each position offering a greater release than the last. The moment that had been building was going to arrive. No stopping it now.

He faced her then. Back in each other's arms, they continued their last, short stretch of lovemaking, falling abruptly off the face of the earth together. It was a powerful fall.

At the bottom, they rested in each other's arms. The acrid smell was gone, replaced by love. Maybe, it took their loving union to cleanse his pores, to renew their life, their future, once again.

He lay on his back, holding her like a treasure. After a few minutes, completely still and resting in his arms, she slipped quietly into a peaceful sleep. He eventually nodded off, too. The world outside had faded from view, for now.

Free Spirit

It has come to my attention
You are not bent on convention
That deserves a reverent mention
To the world.

Though you're not good at addition
It might be - you're on a mission
And, in this life's complete rendition
There's no girl.

For some men, it's an obsession
And I envy your discretion
To not make women a possession
Or a wife.

A spirit free - should roam so
Not be held back, not be tied down so
Should soar up high, and not be forced low
Throughout life.

Your soul is one who's born to travel
So many mysteries to unravel
Yet, judgment slams a gavel
In your face.

Do not listen; do not reason
Enjoy each wild and winsome season
You've committed no high treason
Not a trace.

I've met other people like you
Not enough, so sad, but it's true
Roaming spirits must be free to
Stretch and grow.

To hold tight a bird is so wrong
If I hold tightly or for too long
I'll destroy your joyous, love song
That I know.

Never let them try to change you,
Crush your spirit, rearrange you
Life was not meant to constrain you
I can see.

Take your path where it may lead you
Feel my love whene'er you need to
And in every deed you see to -
Just be free.

Your very spirit does inspire
Your curious nature does desire
Soothing water, searing fire
So, you roam.

May you soar happily ever after
And know that when you leave, your
laughter
Will linger gently in the rafter
Of my home.

A Good Day to Die

He loaded the gun with a single bullet and spun the wheel of fortune, listening to it come to a stop. Was today a good day to die? He wondered.

He was a well-dressed man, sitting in a large, comfortable chair behind a massive cherry desk. Around him, the study was immaculate. Shelves of books lined the walls. A few pieces of art adorned a table here and there.

Dark, elegant, opulent, only the best. He looked around at the understated decadence, his eyes coming to the framed picture sitting on his desk. A tiny spider was crawling across his phone cord. He tore a paper from his notebook and set it down before the spider. It crawled onto the paper and he gingerly carried it, opening the French doors to the patio, and shook it away outside. It was a beautiful day. He inhaled the fresh air deeply and went back and sat down in the study.

Smiling peacefully, he picked up the gun again, put it against his temple and pulled the trigger without hesitation. Click. Nothing. He shrugged his shoulders with a resigned sigh and unloaded the gun, placing it back in his right-hand drawer, and locked it securely. That done, he went out to the patio for breakfast.

The table was set for one. He sat down and unfolded the napkin, placing it on his lap. The morning newspaper was laid out in front of him. As he put on his reading glasses, a servant emerged from inside and began to pour his orange juice.

"Sir, what would you care for this morning?"

"Oh, let's see Gabriel, how about French Toast, no butter or sugar, with a side of fresh fruit. Nothing too heavy on such a beautiful morning."

"As you wish, sir." With that, the man quickly and silently disappeared back into the house.

He browsed through the paper. His stocks were up. A new slew of murders had the south side retreating in fear. The election campaigns were in full swing, with mudslinging in all directions. And there was a sale at Penney's. He chuckled at the allusion and tossed the paper aside.

The breakfast was utter perfection, as it always was. He could set his watch by the arrival of his morning pickup. The car arrived at eight-thirty on the dot. He checked his pocket watch with another amused look and seated himself in the limousine. His secretary was waiting for him inside.

"What's on the agenda today, Coleman?"

"Good morning, sir. Today's schedule, yes. You have a meeting with Palmer and Palmer at ten a.m. Lunch with Gina Mathers, eleven-thirty. Don't know how she arranged that. Gerard's. Two p.m., Derek Waters, Twin Oaks Country Club, a round of golf. Dinner party at Solomon's, six o'clock."

"That's all?"

"Uh, yes sir, that's all, sir." Coleman wasn't sure if that comment had been facetious or not. As relaxed as his boss was, there was something intimidating always lurking. He shifted in his seat.

"This Gina Mathers, tell me more about her. She's lunch?"

"Yes, sir, lunch. Ms. Mathers works for CGA, newly established, looking for backers. The firm uses donations towards helping people of various bad situations move on with their lives: victims of domestic violence, cleaned-up drug abusers, depressives, early widows, displaced homemakers – you name it. All non-profit, focusing within the city limits at present. Hopes to expand. Some big names on board, backing them."

"Yes, yes, all good, of course. Fine then. Ah, we're here."

The car pulled up in front of the stately building and the driver came around to open the door for him. Stepping out of the car, he walked to the entrance. The door was opened for him.

As he went down the hallway to his office, he had to endure at least eight "good morning, sirs" and watched one nervous assistant drop her armful of files as he passed. He smiled, nodded, and proceeded into his suite promptly at nine a.m.

His receptionist followed in behind him and walked directly to the pot of fresh coffee behind the bar. She poured a steaming cup, set it down before him, and closed the double doors behind her as she left. All was quiet again.

He enjoyed the feel of the steam heating up his upper lip and nostrils as he took a drink of coffee. Turning his chair, he peered out the windows at the city. His city.

He'd built an empire so well, it ran perfectly without him. The look of amusement left his face, replaced with a grimace of pain. His eyes squinted and he sipped his coffee, staring into nothing. A buzzer on his desk brought him back to attention.

"Sir, your ten o'clock appointment is here. Dalmer and Dalmer, sir."

"Yes, send them in."

The grimace of pain receded behind the mask. The two men were greeted by a warm smile and a firm handshake. They took their seats, and the meeting began.

"Sir, what you've asked us to do is very unusual. As legal counsel, we found it imperative to meet with you in person. We're sorry to interrupt your busy schedule, but sir, are you sure this is what you want?" He smiled reassuringly at the two uneasy men squirming in their seats.

"Yes, I'm well aware it's an odd request, gentlemen, but I do assure you, it is exactly what I want. Please have it drawn up per my specifications, then send it over to me."

The men looked at each other beseechingly but had no response for someone whose mind was clearly made up. They stood up and shook hands again.

"As you wish, sir. We'll be happy to comply. The papers will be drawn up immediately." They stiffly walked from the room, barely able to contain their bewilderment until the double doors closed again.

The clock read merely six minutes after the hour. Nothing to do until lunch. Again.

Such a busy schedule on paper, so boring in life. Maybe he needed a vacation.

He could herd cattle at a ranch, build bridges to connect the uncivilized parts of the world, bag sand for the impending flood he saw on television.

But they wouldn't let him. No one would ever hear of him doing physical labor. It seemed blasphemous, sacrilegious. What a hypocrisy. What an irony. What a joke, but the joke was on him.

His car delivered him to the restaurant moments before eleven-thirty. Gina Mathers was a well-dressed woman who'd obviously worked her way up from middle-class society. He had keen observation skills.

Wearing a navy business suit, she had dark brown hair, pulled back into a French roll, short, clean nails, and a good handshake. At least, she had him intrigued. They sat at a table in the corner, away from the incoming lunch crowd.

"I'm so glad you accepted this meeting. I was told it's hard to get through to you, and you don't accept invitations from fledgling companies with people like me at the helm."

"Really? And what kind of people are people like you?"

"Well, basically...," she hesitated, "nobodies sir. I'm not even sure how I got this meeting arranged. I called several times and the receptionist politely told me to go away. " He nodded for her to continue.

"Each time I got another backer, I'd try to use the name to get credibility with her. We're trying to do a good thing here. I couldn't get anywhere. And your backing would help us so much."

"Tell me what happened, Ms. Mathers? How did you get through?"

"Gina's fine, really. One day I called, and a man's voice answered. I asked him if he was the new receptionist. He laughed and said no, just a temp filling in. She'd had a dental appointment. I told him of the situation, and he said he'd ask you about it."

"Ah, I see."

"Within just a few seconds, he told me it was all right and set up the appointment. You see, I don't know how I got through, but I did."

He smiled at her, thinking of the day Joyce was having dental pain and he sent her straight away to his own dentist, listening to no arguments from her. The day that he'd had control of the phone.

"Well, then, a stroke of luck for you. You got me here. Now, what can I do for you? I understand CGA helps turn around people after unfortunate situations, domestic violence and the like?"

"Yes, exactly. We offer funds to those trying to start over. There's not a list of qualifications, per se. So many people have different stories. There aren't any right or wrong answers, just an explanation of the circumstances and a demonstration of intent to turn things around. The people are followed closely to make sure they adhere to the requirements set. If they don't, the grant is rescinded. We're doing well, so far."

"Sounds admirable."

"We've had donations from many interested people, but your name on that list would give us the power to increase our credibility and donor base. I know I'm taking your time, and it's valuable, but this program is valuable too. Please, at least consider what you could do for people who are out there struggling, right now."

"Well, Ms. Mathers... Gina. You seem level-headed and off to a good start. I'd be happy to help you. Just get in touch with my accountant, Dave Mason, after tomorrow and he'll work it out with the lawyers."

He wrote down the number and passed it to her. "I'll send him the go ahead and we'll get something arranged. Now, shall we eat?"

"Thank you, sir. Thank you so much. Yes, let's do, if you have time." She smiled gratefully at him.

After a nice meal, and pleasant small talk with her, he asked, "What have you heard about me, if you don't mind my asking. You can't be from around here. You must have moved here recently. You know, you're one of the few people I've met who's not completely terrified of me."

"The truth, sir?"

"Yes, of course, by all means." He motioned for her to continue.

"Well, as for me, I moved here a year ago. You were right. And about you, well..., the story goes like this. You were a happily married man with two children. Several years ago, your family was killed by a drunk driver who crossed the intersection and hit their car head-on. People say it destroyed you, though you don't show it.

Since then, you've never dated. You've mostly been a recluse between home, work, and necessary social functions. You're always calm and relaxed, but you have a sense of power that people find intimidating." She looked at him worriedly, wondering if she should have been so honest. He smiled at her and took her hand.

"Thank you, Gina. Thank you for your candor. And your lack of fear. It's very refreshing to me." He took his hand away, nodded, and sipped his water. His driver appeared at the table and told him it was time to leave for his two o'clock appointment. For once, time had passed too quickly.

"It's been a pleasure, Gina. Please, keep me posted. Let me know if I can be of any more help." With a smile, he turned and left for his meeting at the golf course. Business as usual.

The next morning, he promptly called his accountant and arranged for a donation to CGA. Ten million dollars. He smiled to himself. "That should hold her for a while."

Taking the gun from his drawer, he loaded one bullet and spun it around in the chamber. Was today a good day to die? Putting the gun to his head and squeezing, he heard only a click. He sighed.

Replacing the gun in his drawer, as always, he went out to breakfast. He passed the day, watching the second-hand counting time down in his office. Another day passed at an excruciatingly slow rate.

A week later, he came home from another boring day at the office and went to his study. For some reason, he couldn't get that Gina Mathers out of his mind.

He was thinking about her again as he went to his study. Coming around to take a seat, he noticed the right-hand drawer had been forced open. Bullets were scattered out of the box and the gun was missing.

He looked up to see a man nervously wielding the gun at him from across the room in the shadows.

"It's all your fault. I could have gotten a lesser sentence. It was an accident. I never meant to kill anybody." He shook the gun back and forth as he spoke.

"Michael Conrad," he said evenly. "What brings you here? I thought you were still in prison for killing my family."

"I was, man. I got out. I got out of that joint. You smug piece of shit! Do you know what it's like in prison? Do you know what they did to me? I'm not a criminal, man. I'm in there with killers, see? Killers and psychos. I'm not a killer, man. I got drunk. I hit a car. It was an accident"

He was enraged. His hand continued to shake as he yelled. "Then I read about this thing in the paper! Ten million dollars to help rehab people, give people a second chance. You never gave me a second chance, you piece of shit. You had them throw the book at me! You've got power, man! And you used it. It's your fault. But guess what? Guess who has the power now, asshole?" He shook the gun.

"Michael, Michael, Michael." Moving into the room and away from the desk, he nodded to the drawer. "Better see for yourself."

Confused, Michael backed along the wall towards the desk.

"What do you mean, see for myself? This better not be some kind of trick! Because I've got the gun. I'm in charge! See? I'm in charge! "He peered down into the drawer. "What? What am I supposed to see?"

"Michael, would you believe my family was everything to me? My reason for living. That I would have gladly been in the car, instead of them, but I wasn't given the choice? That my life ended that day?" He nodded at the drawer and continued. "For four years, every morning, I've loaded that gun with one bullet, spun the chamber, put it to my head and pulled the trigger."

"You're full of it, man! You expect me to believe you did that every day since they died, and you're still here? What are the chances of that, huh?"

"Every day since you were put behind bars, but that's exactly what I mean, Michael. What are the chances of that? You see, if you knew about guns and bullets, you'd know. They're blanks. If I'd used real bullets, I'd have been dead fifty-seven times already. I've kept track. It's all there in the notebook."

He nodded towards the drawer again. "You see, I didn't really want to die. I just didn't want to go on living either. It was merely an amusement for me, a way to pass the time. I wondered every morning when I put a bullet in the gun… was it a good day to die?"

He stared at Michael as he continued.

"

Would that have been the day I'd meet my wife and family again? Would I ever see them, or would there be nothing after death? Are they up there somewhere, or simply gone? Forever. Gone from me. Taken from me."

"Shit!" Michael put the gun down on the desk, exasperated, and started pacing to the wall, and then back. "Shit! What kind of stupid fuck are you? I'm not that fucked up!" Michael paced some more. "Shit!" he stopped in the corner.

"What do you want from me? Forgiveness? Absolution?"

He looked questioningly at Michael.

"I want your help! You can fix it. You've got the power. You can fix it. You can change things around for me!"

"You took my wife!" He quietly shouted, then restrained himself.

"I told you I didn't mean to!"

"You took my children."

"It was a fucking accident, man! I was drunk! I didn't mean to kill nobody. You think I wanted to kill somebody? Wanted to go to prison? Fuck no, man! That place is a hole. I wanted outta there!" He continued to go in circles. "Shit."

Michael paced more, back and forth, over and over, finally stopping in the corner. "So why do you have this bleeding heart with everyone else? What about me? What about a second chance for me?"

He stared at Michael, standing there screaming, and a thought occurred to him. Breathing in deeply, he sighed as he let it out. He began by speaking softly and resolutely.

"You're right, but of course you are. I should have seen it. Here I am, helping others get a second chance. Why not you? After all, like you said, it was an accident."

Michael nodded.

"After all this time, it still hurts me like it was yesterday. Seeing their bruised faces, their lifeless bodies. I need closure. It's time for me to do something."

He came around the desk, looking directly into Michael's eyes as he spoke. "I can help you, Michael, you're right. And I will help you, in any way I can. I can see now just how sorry you are." He opened his arms as a show of a truce, after years… years of bitterness, anger, and hatred. Michael's nervous demeanor relaxed a bit.

"You mean it? You'll help me?"

"Yes, I will." Michael walked slowly from the corner of the room to the desk.

He breathed a sigh of relief and relaxed as they stood facing each other, then opened his arms. The sound of the gun's explosion boomed through the night air as the force of the bullet ripped into Michael's chest.

With a momentary look of confusion, Michael fell to his knees, then crumpled to the floor in pain. "Wha...?"

"They weren't blanks. That didn't even make sense. Blanks wouldn't have done much for my health, either, had one shot me in the head. As I said, if you knew anything about guns, you'd know."

Michael was fading but looked up confused.

"You see, Michael, a thought occurred to me while I was over there. The police would have never believed I'd killed you in self-defense if I had shot you from over ten feet away. As I said, and I truly meant, I could see just how 'sorry' you are."

He shook his head at Michael, bleeding out on the floor.

With complete calm, he set the gun back on top of the desk and picked up the phone.

He dialed the operator.

"I'd like the number for Gina Mathers, please. Yes, please connect me. Gina, hello, you got my check, I see. There was a write-up in the paper. Oh, that's quite all right. As you said, it's for a good cause. People everywhere need a second chance."

He glanced to his floor where Michael had fallen and eyed his lifeless body. Blood staining his shirt had pooled on the floor.

His attention switched back to the phone.

"Say... what are you doing for lunch on Friday? I have some things to take care of before then. Great. How about Gerard's again, same time? Wonderful, Gina, I look forward to seeing you. No, no. I really mean it. Okay, I'll see you then."

He hung up the line. Time to put the other things in order.

Staring at his wife's picture on the desk, he nodded to her absently and touched her face with his fingertip.

"I'll guess I'll see you when I see you, love. Kiss the children for me."

He took the picture off of his desk and carried it over to a table, placing it by another photograph from a time long gone by.

"One last detail to take care of, one last loose end," he thought.

Returning to the desk to put closure on this chapter, once and for all, he picked up the phone and dialed the police.

About the Time

About the time you're thinking
Everything's okay
The world around – turns upside down
And steals your breath away.

Paralyzed, you sit and wait
For order to return
And try to pay attention
To the lesson you should learn.

But lessons don't come easy
They can cut you to the bone.
The pain can be unyielding
And you'll feel quite alone.

About the time you're thinking, then
That everything's gone wrong
Your wrong–side world gets righted
You begin to feel strong.

The world seems less unfriendly
Things begin to fall in place
About the time you thought that
Nothing ever went your way.

Everything is easy
Life is smoothly rolling by.
Then, it comes crashing down around you
And takes you for another ride.

Carson and Lindsay

It started out as a chance meeting in a large room full of people and we just noticed each other, conversed, really got along. We stayed in contact and talked through some projects. It was an odd match, I admit. He was wealthy, powerful, and handsome. I was poor, powerless, and plain. That didn't seem to matter, because I could see his heart and he could see my mind.

We'd travel together on projects, where teams were involved, and one day, years into this arrangement, things shifted when a hotel didn't have two rooms available. They only had a small suite with an extra fold-out couch. I was flexible and said that would be fine. We actually got to work together in a closer way, and we took turns cooking food in the kitchenette.

Weeks went by. We were sitting with Jake when a voluptuous and slightly snide team-member sat in the fourth chair at our table and said, "Carson, why are you still making Lindsay sleep on the fold-out couch in your suite? They were only full during that one convention. It was weeks ago. There are plenty of rooms, now."

I panicked. I had no idea what to say, sitting there beside him and, worse, I had no idea what he would say. Truth be told, it took him a minute. Slowly, he looked at her, smiled contentedly, and said, "Thanks, but I think we're good." She seemed a bit taken aback. I couldn't figure that out right away. Why would she care? I can be a bit slow on the uptake.

Then, I looked at him, and at her. Her puzzled look ran from him to me and she just shook her head. She touched the back of his hand gently and moved her fingers in slow circles. Oh, *now* I got it. He was incredibly sexy. That was why.

I said, "Carson is always free to split us back into two rooms, should he want to have a sex lair." She about choked at how direct I was. He turned and looked at me like I'd lost my mind. He was about to speak to that when he saw how embarrassed she was at being called out and pulled her hand away from his.

He got it now, too, and rolled his eyes. "Oh my God, no, I am not looking to have members of the team or the townsfolk coming… to my room."

"Or *in* your room," I added, rolling my eyes.

He grimaced and looked at her. "Not ever." Then he looked back at me. "Lindsay stays, I hope."

I nodded casually and the conversation was a done deal. We were going to move on, and I hoped she was, too.

But then her thoughts hit me, and I was so angry and hurt and reeling. There's this thing I didn't tell you. Sometimes, with people, especially negative people, their thoughts seep into my head and attack me. I'd never told Carson about this and I never could read him at all, probably because he wasn't negative.

But this lady, this fucking snide lady. She thought, "Are they doing it? Is *he* doing *her*? I mean, gross.'" How dare her. I know I shouldn't have spoken up, but I couldn't stop myself. I just became unleashed as I stood up and threw down my napkin. Seething with sarcasm, I completely snapped like a lunatic and that's what I looked like because I was the only one at the table who could hear a person's thoughts.

"As to that, yes! Yes, we *are* an item. In fact, every evening between five and six p.m., we stand on our balcony, naked, and he holds my hips and does me from behind. That way, we can both wave at passers-by. I've been practicing my *queen wave,*" I basically spit out. I demonstrated and waved at her like Queen Elizabeth. "Oh, and fuck you."

I stormed off and heard Carson laugh out loud as he leaned to Jake. "Oh my god, I never even knew Lindsay could get mad. Where did that come from? Funny, though. Queen wave."

The lady said, "I didn't even say that out loud."

Carson caught that and said, "Wait. What exactly did you say in your mind?"

She stared at him. "It's not like she could. It wasn't." She sighed. "I just wondered if you were dating someone like, you know, her... if you two had a weird thing. And I said would you do *her*? Gross."

Carson looked horrified. He said, "My sex life is 100% off limits. It's not a discussion topic. This conversation is done. Leave." She knew when to cut her losses.

He sat there, mulling over what just happened and Jake and he exchanged surprised glances.

"She heard her think that?" Jake asked.

"Maybe it was written on her face. I wasn't looking. She might have sneered like… like Lindsay was beneath me or something."

"Maybe. That made my arms get goosebumps."

Carson smiled. "Yeah, no doubt. See you tomorrow."

He got up and left the dining room, then came and found me. I was sitting in the suite in a recliner, and it had gotten dark. I was kind of dazed, hugging my knees to myself, wondering why people were… like they were.

He walked over in the shadows, picked me up, and carried me to the bed. Setting me upright against the pillows, he kicked off his shoes then crawled over to the middle. Propping up more pillows, he leaned back then pulled me over, simply hugging me against his chest.

Finally speaking, he said, "She was an idiot. I liked the queen wave thing. Funny."

He rubbed my back and kissed the top of my head. I moved my hand slowly down his chest to his ribs, then stopped. I realized if I moved it back up, it would have been an obvious caress. Damn it. Leaving it on his ribs, I would have just been repositioning my hand.

I painfully forced myself not to move it until his breathing evened out. I looked up. I could picture him leaning down as I looked up and gently kissing me. I couldn't help he didn't see me that way and had the choice of nearly every living human. The world was his oyster, but right now, I was in his arms.

I moved my hand back up his chest and he didn't notice. My breath caught and my heart pounded. I moved my hand down and back up then down his arm. My breathing quickened. I needed to stop this right now. I rested my hand on his bicep.

If he knew I was in love with him, would he be disappointed? I was the one person he could count on.

He had sycophants everywhere, but I had always spoken the truth, seen the real him, given him Tums or Immodium. We'd been able to have complete trust, comfort, talk on any subject, do each other's laundry, work together, live life.

What if he found out I was no better than any of them? I could never tell him how I felt because he'd think I'd been shallow all along. I sighed.

I knew the only way to keep him was to keep it work-related and platonic. I could be his friend and colleague, but no more.

I don't know how much time passed but I closed my eyes and my breathing melted into his. And, at some point, I rested.

I didn't see him open his eyes, look at my right hand on his arm, and smile. I didn't feel him close his left arm around me more snugly or move his right hand from my waist to the small of my back.

I didn't know he nuzzled into my hair and sniffed it, kissed my head and smiled, then closed his eyes again.

The Storyteller

The storyteller casts her magic spell
upon the crowd
All ears around are riveted to,
each word she says aloud.

With a gentle, calming voice,
enchanting stories she does tell.
She blends words into a fabric,
no other does it quite so well.

All around the blazing fire,
the circle holds its breath
As she speaks of truth and wisdom,
and of life and love and death.

So enraptured are the lovers,
of the storyteller's words
Their faces lose expression,
with each passing word that's heard.

She lulls them into silence
peaceful, wistful, and content
Their worries long forgotten,
their dreams alive again.

From land to land she wanders,
spreading magic, hope, desire
Looking for explorers,
whose passion she will set afire.

The telling of the tale,
turning phrases like a dance.
Slowly stripping off each veil,
a tantalizing, slow romance.

Carefully crafting words with wisdom,
spinning life out of a dream
Captivating, mesmerizing,
seducing all upon the scene.

Perhaps she'll come to you to visit,
invigorate you with her spirit
Whisper secrets softly to you,
listen closely, you may hear it.

She might caress your soul with comfort,
linger near you for a spell
Share her wisdom with you, knowing,
there are stories you must tell.